LANDSCAPING, MANSCAPING

by Frank Sol

Chapter One

I lifted the tailgate ramp on my trailer to its upright position and snapped the locks into place. Then I rechecked them—I'd to be driving down the road and have the gate drop open when I hit a bump or pothole and have my lawn mowers go rolling out onto the street. Wouldn't do my business much good.

I had my own landscaping service—*Flat Earth Landscaping*—and this late spring was keeping me busy. The early June weather had been cool and wet, for the most part, which meant the lawns were growing really fast and people were scheduling lots of cuts. Today's heat was a surprise, though a pleasant one.

I straightened back up and stretched out my back with a tired groan. I used the sleeve of my navy blue tee-shirt to wipe the sweat from my forehead.

I walked around the trailer, checking to make sure that my two lawnmowers, weed eaters, plastic gas cans, and other tools were fastened in place. The dark green tarp covering the grass clippings and pruned branches in the bed of my *Ford* pick-up was also tied firmly in place.

I opened the cab door and climbed in.

I kept a small cooler in there, stocked with bottles of water and packets of *Crystal Light*. The freezer packs kept everything chilled for the day. I hated drinking lukewarm water, almost as much as I hated plain water. It had to be icy cold...the flavour packs were a bonus.

I still had a *Royal Gala* apple in there too so I munched on it while I checked for messages on my cell phone. Nothing of interest...no one had called while I was working. I flipped the phone to access the day planner and double check the address for my next assignment.

* * *

It was late afternoon when I finally pulled into my driveway. The driveway was the main reason I had bought the house—it was a flattened U-shape, allowing me to drive in off the street and follow the curve back towards the road, but then stop and back the trailer into the garage to store it at night.

After seven years there, I was getting good at backing up.

I stopped the truck and climbed out of the cab. I'd spent money on the garage, having it modified and extended so that it would fit both my trailer and the pick-up. I didn't want to have to unpack it every night—I wouldn't risk leaving my tools out all night for anyone to pick up and steal. Better to just lock the whole trailer up safely.

Having a garage big enough to store the pick-up as well was a bonus—most weekdays I didn't even bother unhooking it from the trailer. Just park it at day's end and forget about it.

I stretched out my arms, feeling the dull ache in my muscles which echoed a most productive day.

Carrying the cooler, I left the garage through the main door. Moments later, it automatically closed and locked. I walked up the flagstone path towards my front door. I could have gone inside through the garage, but I wanted to check for mail—I was expecting cheques from several of my clients.

There was another good reason to walk around the front of the house. The neighbors were home again—after spending a week away at a relative's cottage. While pulling in, I had seen Michael Carmicheal and his daughter, Sarah, unloading boxes and bags of groceries from their station wagon. It was one sight I never got tired of watching.

Mike was a tall man in his late forties, and very hunky, in my opinion. He had short-cropped rust-coloured hair just starting to show a few strands of gray, and big brown eyes. As I rounded the corner of the house, he was bent over, reaching deep into the wagon for the last few grocery bags.

I stopped in mid-step and licked my lips. Mike's dark green *Old Navy* tee-shirt was riding up and his blue *Levi's* were riding low and I could see a nice expanse of lower back, as well as a few inches of plaid flannel boxers. It was a really nice sight—I could feel dick twitch inside my own *Wranglers.*

He straightened up—Sarah had just something to him—and he turned his head, spotted me, and waved. He had a big grin on his face too. It made him look boyish.

I waved back. "Afternoon, Mike." I set the cooler down and walked across the street towards him. "Hi, Sarah."

"Afternoon, Scott." He abandoned the task of unloading the station wagon and met me at the end of his driveway. "Keeping busy?"

"Oh yeah." I nodded my head. "It's the season, right? More work coming in than I can keep up with." *Damn,* I thought. *He looked just as good from the front as he did from behind. Maybe better.* It was so unfair that he was as straight as the proverbial arrow. *One night I'll get you drunk and alone and naked in my bed.* I'd been jerking off to that particular fantasy for years. It would never happen—he was devoted to Jessica, his wife of twenty-some years—but I certainly enjoyed thinking about it. "How're things with you?"

"Good."

"Had fun at the cottage?"

"Yep." He nodded. "We've got it pretty much set up for the summer. Janeen and Loren were happy we could help them out."

"There's always a lot of work left over from the winter."

"Nothing major this year, thank God. Last year was a real bitch."

"I know." I remembered it all too well. A tree had fallen during one of the winter storms so their first visit to his brother-in-law's cottage had involved replacing windows and part of the roof.

"We'll have to take you up with us sometime."

"Loren's that desperate for a decent landscaper?" I laughed and Mike joined in. I'd seen the cottage and 'natural wilderness garden'. *I wouldn't trust Loren to mow a lawn, let alone look after a garden.* "You seem to have brought a lot of food home with you. How much did you take up?"

Mike glanced back over his shoulder. Sarah was still carrying bags into the house, and shooting glares at her father. "We ate most of what we took up. But yeah, we have to restock."

"Seriously, how much did you guys eat?"

"A lot—Loren made us work it off though." Mike's grin grew bigger. "Anyway, we're getting in a good store of food for the next few weeks. Special event after all."

"Throwing a party?"

"Yeah, next Friday night. Jason is coming home."

My eyes grew wider. "He is?"

"Yep." Mike now had a huge smile on his face. "Finally got back over here safe and sound. And, even better, he's out."

"Damn. That *is* good news."

"It is."

I smiled at him, matching his eager grin. His son, Jason, had been stationed overseas for months. It was good to hear that he was back home safely...and it would be even better to see him in person.

From what I remembered of emailed pictures and one or two visits before he had shipped out, Jason looked amazing in his uniform.

Nothing like a young hunky man in uniform—any uniform.

It would be nice to see him back, I thought. I could feel my dick twitch inside my jeans. *Down boy.* Jason had always looked like a younger, even hunkier version of his father. He'd always had that 'all-American, mid-west, corn-fed, healthy, red blooded, young man' look, for all that he was born and raised in Canada.

After saying good-bye to Mike, and leaving him to help Sarah finish carrying in the groceries, I scooped up my cooler and ducked inside my own home. I tossed the mail onto the coffee table, walked past the dining room, and into the kitchen. I threw the freezer pack into the freezer to refreeze for tomorrow and then rinsed out the cooler in the sink and left it in the dish drainer to drip.

There were no messages waiting on my answering machine, which was a good thing. I hadn't expected anything to be waiting for me. I already had more clients than I could keep up with, on my own, and most of my friends were out of town.

The house was large for just me living there, but I had bought it for the beautiful backyard, the driveway, and the space. I used part of the ground floor as my business office—why rent space somewhere? The room might have been meant as a den, or a bedroom, but it was a perfect office space for me, with a window looking out into my backyard.

The backyard was a beautifully laid out. I had a small fountain set in a small cobblestone courtyard. I could listen to the fountain gurgling through the open window when I was working in my office during warm weather. There were trees to provide shade, a nice expanse of manicured lawn, and small flower beds and a vegetable garden.

My friends were often surprised at just how much landscaping there was in my yard. They thought I'd be tired of gardening. I did that for a living, why would I want to have more to do at my own home?

I enjoyed it...always had. Simple answer.

I unhooked my cell phone off my belt and set in on my desk. I'd have to do some bookkeeping later.

Right now, I wanted a hot shower.

Going upstairs and into the *en-suite*—I had three bathrooms in the house though I tended to use this one most of the time—I lifted my sweaty tee-shirt over my head tossed it into the laundry chute. Then I unzipped my jeans and pushed them down my legs. I tossed them into the chute, along with my cotton boxers.

I reached for the shower taps, then paused. Standing there naked, I looked at myself in the mirror.

I had a good body. It was muscular—from my career choice, not from being a gym-bunny—and covered with hair. I trimmed my chest and pubes—I refused to shave it off, but I'd been told that a little manscaping made me look more desirable. My dark brown hair was always kept short. My green eyes were a bit watery and I thought that my nose was over-large, but I couldn't do much about it. I already had a good tan colouring my skin—basically the only pale white skin was covered by my boxers; yeah, it was May, but I worked outdoors. I also worked shirtless on some jobs—lonely housewives enjoyed the show—and definitely dressed in as little as possible while looking after my own yard.

And my dick was standing at attention.

Given my memories about how hot and seriously fuckable Jason had looked in his uniform, I had grown hard. Now, I was getting harder. *Why yes, I do love to salute our troops.* Having already removed my boxer shorts, my hard-on was now free to flop around. I reached down and gave it a few gentle strokes.

I stepped into the tub, under the warm jet of the shower spray, letting the glass door swing shut behind me. The water felt really good pounding against my shoulders and back.

I lathered up, rubbing the washcloth across my chest. I ran the cloth across the rest of my body, taking special care to wash the sweat and dirt from every inch.

My dick responded, growing harder. I squeezed some bodywash gel into my hands, rubbing them to work up a good lather, and then I took my erection in both hands. I was stroking it, playing with it. The friction was just right, feeling so good.

I could feel myself getting even harder, getting closer to cumming.

I kept rubbing, using both hands to stroke my shaft. My eyes were closed and I was picturing Jason in his army uniform. There was this one picture I had seen on *Facebook* and printed out a copy of—he was wearing desert camouflage pants, his brown tee-shirt and hair both dark with sweat, and he had a huge grin on his face, and a lump in his pants. He had just finished wrestling with some of the guys in his barracks and he looked more like he had just finished foreplay. That picture made him look so fucking hot.

And it was all the stimulation I needed.

I grunted and felt my knees buckle as I shot my load. Ropey strands of cum splashed across the shower tiles, quickly washing away under the pounding spray. I slumped against the tiles myself.

Chapter Two

I flipped open my laptop, then walked back to the kitchen to pour myself a fresh mug of coffee—I needed at least two mugs in the morning to get my brain awake and working. Returning to the living room, I found that my laptop was booted up and ready.

I took a sip of coffee and proceeded to click through a couple of newspaper websites to read the day's headlines. There wasn't much of anything interesting there. The usual bad news and a lot of drivel about so-called superstars. I mean, seriously, who gave a fuck that some singer had cut his hair? I grunted and clicked away. These people made more money in a year than I'd make in my lifetime.

I updated my cell phone's day planner with the day's jobs. A quote for redoing a front yard was the first thing; I'd start with it at nine so that I was still fresh and clean. Then I had five lawns to mow and a backyard pond to clean out.

I skimmed through a couple of my favourite picture-heavy websites, getting myself all worked up. I stood up, the front of my faded blue jeans bulging out. As usual, I'd given myself a serious hard-on by looking at those pictures. I'd have to take care of it before leaving for work.

I had one more day of work before the weekend. It would be a relatively light day...only six houses to look after, though that pond job was going to be a mucky one.

Next week the schedule got more brutal. *Maybe I should think about hiring some help. Put an ad in the paper for a college student or two.* Cute, clean-cut college boys working up a sweat in the sun, dressed in shorts and tee-shirts...

Feeling my dick throb painfully in my jeans, I pushed the laptop away.

The front of my jeans were tented out, the worn-in denim outlining my hard-on for anyone to see. Not that anyone else was around.

I pushed up my red stripped polo shirt, pulling it over my head and tossing it onto the couch—I'd planned to wear it to the business meeting, then change to a plain tee afterwards. I reached down and unzipped my jeans. My hard dick popped through the fly of my boxers. I started stroking myself.

I was imagining that I had gotten Mike drunk. I had always wanted to get him naked—seeing him in just a pair of soaked swim trunks when we camped at the lake was just a big tease—and I wanted to find out just how much he took after his younger brother. So far, he had proved elusive to my stalking and....

A cab pulled up in front of Mike's house.

I pulled the curtain back a bit so that I could look outside. I was still stroking myself, feeling my hard-on throbbing in my hand. I knew no one outside could see what I was doing.

A young man was pulling a pair of duffle bags out of the taxi's trunk.

When he straightened up, I could see his face.

Jason Carmichael was even hotter now. He looked more like his uncle than his father. Looked like just like a twenty year old Alec in fact.

Damn, I thought, my mouth hanging open. My dick twitched in my hand and then I came.

* * *

I had first met up with Alec Carmichael in college. We shared a couple of classes in our first year and we both kept running into each other at the gym and at various parties. For whatever reasons, we ended up in the same social circle. In our second year, we decided to rent an apartment together—neither of us could afford to rent one alone and there were plenty of other expenses to pay. Better to make your plans and pick a room-mate you liked, than risk going the school random assignment system.

In the first year, I'd thought that Alec set off my gaydar on more than one occasion, but I wasn't completely sure. He talked about girls, though he never seemed to take anyone home from the various parties we'd attended. But then, neither did I...though we both talked up a good deal about our supposed conquests. While hanging in his dorm room, I had thought about snooping through his computer to check out which websites he frequented—his computer browsing history would be a clear sign to his sexual preferences—but he never left his laptop unlocked.

Of course, in that first year I was still hiding my own sexuality and kept my own internet browsing as much of a secret. I don't think Alec knew that I was gay—I don't think anyone knew.

Once we became roommates, I thought things would change.

Whether or not, Alec knew that I was gay, he certainly seemed to enjoy teasing me. He usually stripped down after classes to relax, spending most of his time in either tight *Hanes* boxer briefs or else in brightly patterned boxer shorts that showed me tantalizing hints at the shape and size of his cock. I could see it flopping around when he walked through our apartment or was sprawled on the couch to watch television. After showering, especially on a weekend, he'd saunter around with just a towel wrapped loosely around his waist. He liked flaunting his body.

I liked watching him flaunt.

I'd pray that the towel would slip and give me a good look at him.

With that as my example, I loosened up as well. I'd saunter around in just my boxers as well, though I was less circumspect than wearing just a towel. I had a good body—plenty of time in the gym and out running—so I knew I had no reason to hide. I also hoped that seeing me half-naked would spark something from him...maybe encourage him to try and make a move on me.

Sadly, it never did.

After about two months, I had landed a part-time job, working some evenings and most weekends at this coffee shop downtown. Extra money for school, and a chance to see some friends during the literary readings. Yah, the coffee shop had pretensions and would cater to the city's literary types. Come in on a Saturday night and listen to live poetry or book readings, take part in lively debates, and drink lots and lots of coffee. It was fun.

Friday nights were usually early ones for me as I worked long shifts on pretty much every Saturday. Well, not always early...some nights I chose to go out partying with my friends and would just have to suffer through the next day at work.

I looked forward to these weekend shifts, because I enjoyed the poetry nights, but also because I got to work with the hottest guy I'd ever seen.

Jeremy was blond, with a wrestler's build, and every now and then I got to peek at him when he was changing clothes in the employee restroom. Once, I'd even stood next to him at the urinal and watched him shake a nice piece of uncut meat before he tucked it away again. As soon as he left the restroom, I ducked into a stall, locked the door, and blew a quick load just thinking about what I'd like do with his body.

And he was the boss's son.

So not much chance of my ever risking an encounter with him. He seemed straight, hit on the girls who worked with us, and flirted shamelessly with the customers.

It was a subtle torture...two hot guys I saw on a regular basis and never a chance to hit on either of them.

So another Friday evening night had come and gone in its typical quiet fashion. I had the apartment to myself—Alec had gone out. I used the time wisely. I finished off an assignment that was due on

Monday, and watched part of a new horror series on the television. I checked my emails one last time—nothing of interest—and then locked the laptop and retired to my bedroom and climbed into bed.

I was just on the edge of falling asleep when I heard the apartment door open and what sounded like two people coming inside.

One of the voices was Alec's, and the other sounded vaguely familiar. I couldn't quite place it though.

Who the hell? I thought as I laid there. The second voice didn't sound like it belonged to any of our usual friends. *Who did he bring home?*

I tossed the blankets back and got to my feet.

I opened the bedroom door a crack and looked down the hallway.

I'd left the fluorescent over the stove burning in the kitchen, and it threw light into the hallway. I could see Alec and another guy standing there, just inside the doorway, locked in a passionate embrace.

Well, I thought, *that answers* all *my questions about Alec.* I licked my lips...just watching those two making out was gonna give me fodder for months of future jerk-off sessions.

They moved away from the door, turning enough so that I could see the other guy's face.

Now I knew why the other voice was familiar—the other guy was Jeremy Wilkonson! I worked with him at the coffee shop—his father was the owner!

The two men stumbled into the living room, practically falling onto the couch. They were still kissing and groping at each other. I could hear them moaning and muttering softly to one another.

Within moments, they had pulled off each other's shirts, followed by dropping their jeans, and then Alec got down on the floor in front of Jeremy and began mouthing his hard cock through the fabric of his tight briefs.

Still standing behind my bedroom door, I now had my own rapidly stiffening cock in my hand and was stroking it inside my boxers while watching Alec suck on Jeremy's own beautiful hard-on.

After a few minutes, Jeremy pulled Alec back up onto the couch and then he slipped his briefs down his legs, pushing Alec's boxer briefs down to the floor. Alec went face-down over Jeremy's fat, uncut cock, slurping noisily at it. Jeremy lay back, settling deeper into the couch. He placed his hand on the back of Alec's head, pushing him down, and thrusting himself into the other man's mouth. Alec choked a bit. Jeremy let up on him, but continued forcing his head down on that big cock. Alec was clearly loving it.

I shifted position, knocking my knee against the door.

Jeremy looked up.

Alec sucked sucking.

They'd heard me.

I stood paralyzed as Alec got up and slowly walked down the hallway to my door as Jeremy stood watching. I was mesmerized by the sight of Alec's naked body. His hard-on was bouncing with every step.

Alec pushed my door open. "So," he growled, "you enjoying the show?"

My mouth was open, but no sounds were emerging.

Alec glanced down.

There was no missing the bulge which tented out the front of my boxers. Or the fact that my hand was inside them.

"Get out here." With that, he pulled me out of my room and dragged me to the living room. "Stand right there."

So there I was, standing in front of a completely naked and hard coworker wearing nothing but my boxer shorts, my still-hard cock sticking through the fly.

Jeremy smiled wickedly at me. "You never showed me all *that* at work, Scott," he said. "Trying to hide it?"

"You know each other?"

"He works at the coffee shop," Jeremy explained.

"Jeremy is the boss's son," I said at the same time.

"Cool." Now Alec was smiling too. "Scott, why don't you get naked?"

He didn't have to ask me twice. I slid my shorts down, feeling my face flush as the movement brought their beautiful hard cocks right in level with my eyes.

Jeremy pushed me to my knees and slapped his fat cock against my face, tracing a slick of pre-cum across my lips, and my mouth opened instinctively. Jeremy wasted no time in filling my mouth with his big cock, and I savored the sweet-salty taste and feel of his skin on my tongue.

Alec stood next to him, stroking his cock with one hand and holding the top of my head to steady it as Jeremy slid in and out of my mouth.

Then Jeremy stepped aside, and Alec's cock replaced his in fucking my mouth. Alec tasted just as nice. He was leaking big-time too.

Jeremy pulled me down onto the couch so I ended up laying on my back, and Alec repositioned himself over my face so I could lick his balls. He would then periodically switch and dip his cock into my mouth instead.

Wow, I thought. *I had no idea he tasted this good.*

Jeremy lifted my legs into the air and started licking my hole—I was glad I had showered earlier—and then he slid in his thick fingers inside, stretching me.

I grunted, caught off-guard.

"You'll love it," Jeremy growled softly. "You've been begging for it at work—I've seen you watching me in the toilet."

Moment later, I felt the burn of that thick cock pushing its way into my ass, and as I cried out, Alec's cock slid into my mouth. I had never been filled from both ends before, and it was amazing being between these two studs. Jeremy began pounding my ass, pushing my whole body forward into Alec's crotch, forcing that long cock farther down my throat. The two of them quickly worked out a rhythm, rocking my body back and forth. I was in heaven between my roommate and my coworker.

When I felt Alec's cock tensing in my mouth, I knew he was about to blow his load. "Shoot it," I mumbled. "I want to taste it."

He misunderstood me—my mouth *was* full after all—and pulled himself out. Before I could protest, he grunted and hot ropes of cum splashed across my face and open mouth. Moaning softly, he dragged his cock across my cheeks and lips, smearing me with more juice. Smiling down at me, he pushed his cock back into my mouth so that I could it with my tongue.

Jeremy began to grunt and thrust himself more powerfully inside me. "You have such a nice tight ass," he said. "I love it." He pulled out, fumbled with a condom, and then shot his own hot, thick cum onto my dick and balls.

I lay there, panting.

Jeremy took a step away and then pulled Alec forward. "Get down there," he snapped. "Clean him up." Pushing the back of his head, he forced Alec's face against my still-hard cock, making him lap up what he had left there.

As Alec continued to lick my cock and balls—sending shivers through my body and making me gasp—Jeremy straddled my chest and worked his cock against my lips and tongue, making me clean off his shaft.

I have to admit, I did enjoy licking his foreskin and tasting myself on him—I'd never had an uncut guy before.

Before long, Alec was sucking my dick outright. It took almost no time before I lost control and spurted my cum into his mouth. I was unable to warn him that I was close—being pinned down by Jeremy.

Jeremy was grinning while he face-fucked me. He kept grinning when he came again, blowing a second load into my mouth. It wasn't as much as he'd shot on my crotch, but I was impressed that he was able to cum again so rapidly.

Eventually, he pulled his dick out of my mouth and climbed off my chest. "You're both good at giving head," he said. He glanced at my roommate.

Alec hurried to the bathroom to grab some towels and a wet facecloth so we could clean ourselves up.

"That was fun. We'll definitely have to do it again sometime." Without another word, Jeremy got dressed and left.

Remaining equally silent until the door closed, Alec gave me a shy smile and then darted into his own bedroom and closed the door.

Frowning, I snagged my boxers up from the floor and headed back to my own bed. I was sure, from the look in Jeremy's eyes that he had future plans for my roommate and I.

I was looking forward to them.

Chapter Three

The weather was good on Friday night for the Jason's welcome home party.

I attended—Mike wouldn't take '*no*' for an answer—and I was enjoying myself. There must have forty or fifty people there. A mixture of relatives and friends, many of whom I knew from previous parties. Mike and Jessica loved to entertain...and they had the house and yard for it.

Mike's backyard was nicely manicured—I had done most of the design work on it, after all, so of course it looked totally amazing. The flagstone patio was sunk partially, so it was surrounded on two sides by the house and on one by a low stone wall. The fourth side was open so you could just walk out onto the grassy yard. There were lots of round flowerbeds—Jessica's pride—and flowering shrubs along the fence.

Jason was present talking to a group of his friends—we'd spoken briefly when I first arrived. He had dressed in a tight tee-shirt and equally tight khaki shorts. The clothes showed off his well-exercised body.

I tried not to stare and drool, but he looked so hot. The pictures I'd seen and lusted over just didn't do him justice. His friends weren't half-bad either...three of the five were well worth a second look. One of them was cute enough that I had almost blown my load just looking at him bent over to pick up a beer can from the ground.

"How's business, Scott?" a voice asked

"It's good, Jessica." I turned away from her son and nodded to her. She was Mike's wife—they were one very happy couple. "Maybe too good."

"Can business ever be 'too good'?" she asked me with a grin.

"It can when I'm being run ragged trying to keep up with it."

"You need staff."

"I know, I know." I really would have to hire someone. "Maybe I should ask some of Jason's friends to come and work for me."

"I don't know if any of them are looking right now," she replied. Then she gave my shoulder a playful swat. "You just want to see them parading around half-naked."

"And you wouldn't?"

"I'd hire them." She laughed—she was just a big flirt. "I need a pool boy."

"You don't have a pool."

"You could put one in for me. Then I could watch you strutting around half-naked."

"And what would your husband think about that?"

"I wouldn't tell him." She laughed again and I joined in.

"What's so funny?" Mike walked towards us in a tee-shirt and shorts. He was carrying a beer bottle in one hand and a wine glass in the other.

Jessica took the wine glass from him. "Just talking business."

"Are you hiring?" Mike asked his wife. "She wants a hunky landscaper to boss around," he told me. "Know anyone you'd care to recommend?"

"Knowing your wife, no." We all laughed.

"Don't you have some meat to burn?" Jessica asked.

Mike nodded. "I yeah, I should throw the burgers on or it'll be dark before we sit down to eat." He wandered towards the barbeque.

"You want a hand?" I asked.

"Sure. Thanks, Scott."

I followed Mike, taking a moment to enjoy the way the cotton of his shorts gripped his ass-cheeks.

"Normally I'd ask Jason to help...but I can hardly make him work at his own welcome home party."

"No, not really." I glanced back at Jason. Yeah, he looked even cuter in person.

Clusters of tikki torches were lit and burning brightly. The citronella in the oil appeared to be working as I hadn't been bothered any mosquitoes so far. Solar lanterns glowed along the fence and candles burned on the tables.

There was a burst of loud laughter from the back corner of the yard.

I glanced that way, but I couldn't see anything. It was just too dark back there.

Jessica had vanished inside the house with Sarah.

Mike was talking with some of his own friends, near the now-cooling barbeque.

A lot of the guests had already left, but some of the die-hard partiers remained. Jason and his buddies were out in the dark garden. I wondered what they were laughing about.

My beer was almost empty. *Do I want another one?* I sighed and lifted my head. *How many of these had I drunk tonight?* I'd lost count.

Jason was walking across the patio towards me. "Hey, Mister Owens. Enjoying yourself tonight?"

"Yeah." I nodded. *Enjoying the view of you too,* I thought, but I managed not to say that part out loud. I picked up my beer off the low stone railing and took another long swallow. There might be one good mouthful left. "You know, Jason," I said, slurring my words heavily. "You look just your Uncle Alec when he was your age."

Jason smiled at that—he shared his uncle's boyish features.

And those beautiful brown eyes, I thought as I took another drink. "He was a great guy." I was gesturing with my now-empty bottle. "A really great fucking guy."

"A pity he couldn't make it tonight."

"I wondered where he was." Alec was hot. Alec was a great fuck. *Maybe it was just as well that he wasn't here.* Alec, Mike, and Jason all in one place might have overwhelmed my commonsense enough for me to try and drag at least one of them into the bushes. Or the bathroom. "He was the life of the party back in college."

"I think you've had enough of that for now." Jason pulled the bottle away from my hand.

"We had a lot of fun back in college," I told him. "The things we got up too..."

"You've told me about them."

"Only some," I pointed out. "We'd go out drinking and then stagger back home so hammered we could barely stand. Hit the bars and then be hit on in return...so many offers to go off someplace for a quick fuck. There was this one time I recall that...hell, you're not old enough to hear all the details yet." My beer-soaked brain had finally caught up to my mouth at that point and I shut up. *He doesn't want to hear about how many times I fucked his uncle!* I really doubted it. *Hey, Jason, let me tell you about how your uncle and I used to make out in our apartment.*

I rose, somewhat unsteadily, to my feet. "I'm making an ass of myself, aren't I?"

"Yeah." Jason was grinning as he nodded his head. "You are making a huge ass of yourself, Mister Owens."

I tried to gather what little remained of my dignity. "I should go."

"You gonna make it home, old man?" Jason asked.

"It's just across the street. I'll be fine." I staggered across the patio, heading towards the gate. "I can make it." I looked around, but I didn't see Mike or any of his friends still outside.

Jason was standing on the patio, watching me.

I waved goodnight.

I staggered back into my house. I was still pretty buzzed and feeling no pain. Buzzed? Hell, I was flying almost entirely on autopilot. Definitely had two many beers tonight.

Staggering upstairs, I managed to pull my tee-shirt over my head and dropped it onto the bedroom floor. I unzipped my shorts and let them fall to the floor as well. I collapsed into bed.

I'd finished my shift at the coffee shop, glancing at Jeremy whenever I thought I could do so unnoticed.

As the day progressed, I was pretty sure that he was watching me and smiling somewhat mysteriously. Yep, I was certain he had plans for us later that night.

When the shift ended, Jeremy disappeared.

Somewhat disappointed, I headed back to the apartment.

The shower was running so flopped onto my bed with a textbook. We had a test scheduled for Monday and I knew that I needed to do a lot more studying if I was going to pass it.

I looked up at a knock.

Alec stood there in the doorway, wearing only a fluffy green towel wrapped around his waist. Drops of water were slowly dripping from his smooth, muscular chest, down his flat stomach, and onto the floor. "Can I borrow your deodorant?" he asked. "I've run out."

I let myself quite noticeably run my eyes up and down his body. My dick twitched when he reached down to scratch himself through the towel. "Yeah, I think I got some." I rolled over, only reluctantly tearing my gaze away from him, so that I could dig through the nightstand.

"Is Jeremy coming back over tonight?'

"I'm not sure," I admitted. "He took off after work. Before I could ask him." I found my tube of deodorant and tossed it to him.

"Damn." Alec caught the deodorant with his left hand. At the same time, his towel slipped from his waist and fell to the floor, leaving him standing there naked. "Oh, shit!" He snatched the towel up and quickly wrapped it back around his waist. "Sorry about that."

"Why be sorry?" I asked. "I mean, after last night..."

He gave me a sheepish grin. "Well...." The towel was beginning to slip again, giving me a flash of his pubes, but he caught it. "You gonna study all night?"

"Maybe. We do have that test coming up."

"I know. I read that book once already. I hate having to slog through it all again."

"We gotta do it though. So...why not study together?"

"Yeah, we could do that. Make this a bit more fun." Alec smiled. He had bright white teeth and a perfect face: square jaw, full lips, large, enticing brown eyes, and a perfect head of short reddish hair.

I smiled too and my dick twitched inside my jeans.

Alec winked. "I'll be back in a second." He turned, letting my door swing half-closed behind him, and headed towards his room.

I unfastened the button on my jeans, reached inside to find my growing hard-on, and gave it a few strokes. *Hmm...Alec in just a towel. Now that was a really nice sight. Not going to help with studying, but it is certainly stimulating!*

The bedroom door swung open and my eyes popped open.

Alec, still wearing just that towel, stepped back into my room.

And Jeremy, dressed in loose track pants and a tee-shirt, followed him.

I snatched my hand away from my crotch and sat upright in my bed. "Jeremy!"

"The front door was open so I let myself in." He was grinning. "Did I interrupt something?"

"Not yet," Alec replied.

"Good."

I licked my lips. Although both men looked different, they were both equally hot. Jeremy's face was more curvy and round; his lips a little thinner, his eyes more serious than Alec's. Alec's body was thicker and more muscular, while Jeremy's body was similar to my own—slim, but toned, with great pecks and even greater set of abs.

"So, I know you like dick." Jeremy pulled his tee-shirt over his head and tossed it onto a chair. "Drop the towel."

Alec looked at Jeremy, and then back at me. Smiling, he unfastened the towel from his waist, and once again it fell to the floor. He was sporting a semi now, and it was rapidly growing harder.

"So you've been lusting after his body for a while, haven't you, Scott."

"Yeah." I could hardly deny it after last night's performance.

Alec was still smiling. Drops of water continued to slide down his fit body and fall to the floor.

"Come on over here, Alec," Jeremy ordered. "Get on your knees and come over here."

To my surprise, Alec did as he was told. He crawled all the way to Jeremy, on his hands and knees.

I was shocked by that. From what I knew about the two of them, I would've picked Alec as the dominating one.

Jeremy stared straight at me, never breaking eye contact as he calmly yanked down his track pants and *Tommy* briefs. "You want a piece of this?" he asked, stroking his uncut dick.

"Yeah."

"You want to see your roomie sucking it?"

"Yeah, I do." I wanted to suck on it myself.

Jeremy looked down at Alec who was still kneeling beside him. "Go ahead."

Alec quickly wrapped his lips around Jeremy's dick.

Jeremy's eyes closed and his mouth partially opened in satisfaction. He grabbed the back of Alec's head, pushing his dick deeper down Alec's throat. "You like sucking my big dick, don't you?"

My own dick was throbbing now, fully aroused and still confined inside my jeans. I had to let it out. I unzipped and snatched it through the fly of my boxers. I stroked myself, enjoying the show.

"Damn, Scott," Jeremy said. "You've got a nice big dick too." He pulled Alec's head back and made him look. "You see that...you want to taste it, don't you?"

Alec nodded.

"Then go suck him off."

Alec crawled over to me, eyes focused on my hard dick. I was already panting—unable to believe that this was happening to me. A year and a half of lusting after Alec and now I was having sex with him again!

"Relax, Scott," Jeremy said, still stroking himself. "You're gonna love this. Your roomie is a great cock-sucker."

Alec grasped my dick tightly with his hand, like he was playing with a video game joystick, and he jerked me off a little. He flicked the tip of his tongue around the head of my dick and licked the shaft.

"Take it all."

Alec obeyed Jeremy, swallowing my dick whole. The inside of his mouth felt so warm and nice on my dick. Alec dragged his lips up and down the length of my shaft. He licked my balls as well, sucking each one into his mouth.

I closed my eyes and arched my back, so that I would go deeper into his mouth.

"How does it feel?" Jeremy asked.

"Fuck me," I murmured, "That feels great."

"You want to fuck?" Jeremy was grinning more broadly now. "Alec, you heard him. He wants to fuck. Stand up."

"But I want to suck his dick some more."

"Later. Scott, finishing taking off your clothes. I want to see all of you."

Now it was my turn to do what I was told.

I pulled off my tee-shirt and tossed it onto the floor. I finished pushing my jeans down my legs, followed by my boxers. I was as naked as the others. And just as hard.

"Get on the bed."

Alec climbed onto my bed, his hot ass in the air, and his head on the pillow.

Jeremy tossed something at me. "Here you go."

I ripped open the condom and slipped it on. I squeezed some lube from the tube and smeared it around Alec's hole.

I pushed Alec's butt-cheeks apart, and slid my dick into his hole.

Alec cried out, but the pillow muffled the sounds. I shoved my dick in, harder this time, and he lifted his head to cry out.

Jeremy was grinning widely. "You both look like you're enjoying yourselves."

"Oh, I am," I replied.

Alec only groaned.

Jeremy walked towards me. He rubbed his big uncut cock against the side of my face. I could feel his sticky juice smeared against my cheek. "Fuck him harder, Scott. I want him to scream louder."

I didn't obey right away.

Alec twisted his neck around so he could look at me. "Do it," he said in a soft voice. "Make me your bitch."

That was all the encouragement I need. I started thrusting myself deeper into his ass with more force. And every time I entered him, I could feel myself getting closer and closer to cumming.

Jeremy watched us, rubbing his dick under my chin, across my cheeks, against my lower lip. I wanted it to be in my mouth, but Jeremy kept pulling it away when I tried to suck him.

Alec was groaning as I pounded him.

"Shoot in his ass," Jeremy ordered. "I want to see the look on your face when you cum all in his ass."

Alec was grunting now, very loudly, and the even the pillow didn't do anything to quiet him.

My entire body shuddered as I finally shot my load. I had my eyes squeezed close and my mouth hanging open.

"Fuck!" Alec cried out at the same time.

Jeremy kept slapping his slimy dick against my face. "Good job, Scott."

I collapsed backwards onto the bed, my dick popping out of Alec's ass.

"A very good job." Jeremy gave his dick a few more strokes. "Uhh!" he grunted as he shot his own load onto Alec's face. "Fuck, that was good."

Alec blinked his eyes, tiredly. Cum was dripping down his face and onto his chest.

I noticed that there was more cum smeared on his stomach and pooling on the bed sheets. *He must have blown his own load while I was fucking him.*

Jeremy pulled the condom off of my now-flaccid dick. He ran his fingers down it, as if squeezing a tube of toothpaste, and squirted my cum onto Alec's hairy chest. "There you go." He had a smile—a cruel smile—on his face. "I'm sure you both loved that."

Alec didn't reply.

Neither did I—I was still recovering from the intense orgasm.

Jeremy reached down and pulled up his briefs and then his track pants. "I wish I could stay longer, but I have to meet friends at the gym." He pulled his tee-shirt on as well. "See you at work, Scott." He rubbed his hand through Alec's hair—the same hand he had used to squeeze the condom. "See you too." He walked out of the room.

Alec looked at me. He looked slightly shell-shocked.

I managed to sit up and gave him a hug.

"What was that for?"

"You looked like you needed it."

"Thanks...I think." Recovering, he pulled himself away from me. "But I'm a mess right now."

"Yeah, so what?" By hugging him, I had gotten cum smeared onto myself. The cum from *three* different guys—it was actually a turn-on. "Want me to wash your back?"

Chapter Four

I woke up, a raging hard-on nearly bursting out of my boxers.

I slid my hand down into my shorts. I gave myself a few strokes, but my heart wasn't really into it. Reluctantly, and slowly, I rolled out of bed.

That much movement was enough for me. Almost too much. My head was pounding. My tongue felt twice its normal size. My eyes were blurry and refused to come into focus.

The curtains were open and I could outside. At least it was overcast today—I really wasn't up to facing a bright sunny day.

I shook my head at how I felt and stopped with a wince. "Urgh," I mumbled. I staggered into the *en-suite* almost falling twice. Leaning on the sink vanity to steady myself, I stared at my face in the bathroom mirror.

"I gotta stop drinking that much," I groaned. I wasn't a young man anymore after all.

I reached for the shower faucets. Hopefully I'd feel better after a hot shower.

The doorbell rang.

I winced, cursing softly. The hot shower had helped...a bit. The third mug of coffee was doing more for me though. I didn't remember drinking the first one, and I barely recalled the second, but I was savoring the third. Maybe I would have some toast in a bit.

Right now, I only wanted more sleep. Peace and quiet and a dark place to rest.

The doorbell rang a second time.

"Damn it!" I rose to my feet and stumbled down the hallway.

I unlocked the front door—had I actually remembered to lock it last night?—and swung the door open.

Jason was standing out on the porch. He was wearing a loose gray tee-shirt and blue nylon shorts. His hair was slicked back and he was clean shaven. "Morning, Mister Owens."

"Morning." I nodded to him. He looked perky...the opposite of how I felt.

"Did I wake you?"

"No, I was just having breakfast." I didn't recall just how much of a fool I had made of myself last night, but I was certain I had said or done something. I usually did, which was why I seldom drank that much. "Come on in."

Jason followed me to the kitchen.

"The party sure was fun last night."

"Yeah, it was." I sat down at the table and took a long drink of the orange juice I'd gotten out of the fridge. I hoped it would help get rid of my hangover more than the coffee had.

"I really enjoyed it. I was glad to see you come over."

"Your father invited me."

Jason had a somewhat sheepish grin on his face—it made him look even more boyish than usual. "I asked if he was going too."

"Oh." I looked at him. He had a flush of color in his cheeks. *Is he still hungover as well?* I wondered.

"Everyone enjoys a good party. I know Mom and Dad did...if they can remember any of it. They drank more than you did last night."

I winced at that.

Jason toyed with the glass of orange juice I'd poured him. "So...I hear that your business is doing well."

"Yeah...almost got more work than I can keep up with." I was still keeping my weekends free, though, and working close to forty hours during the week. *As long as I can,* I thought.

"That's good."

I took another sip of my juice.

"No, it is good to hear that." Jason gave me another look. He obviously had something on his mind. "Always good to know that friends are doing well for themselves. Dad used to email me. Keep me up-to-date on what was happening at home."

"He forwarded a few of the emails around to relatives and friends," I told him. "I saw a few pictures. Watched your posts on *Facebook.*" *Jerked myself off thinking about you in your uniform. The usual.*

"Busy businesses usually need to hire on extra staff. I *am* looking for a job, you know."

I looked at Jason, my jaw dropping open in surprise.

"I'm serious, Mister Owens."

"What about the army?"

"I'm done with the service." He shrugged. "I opted out of reenlisting. One tour was enough for me. Got the money I wanted to earn for school, but now I don't know that I want to attend college. I'm not sure what I actually want to take."

"Oh."

"So, I thought I might work for a while until I make up my mind."

"You're sure about that?"

"Yeah...for now." He paused and took a drink of his juice. "I could sign back up...but I don't want to. I want to try something else."

I frowned. "Landscaping with me?"

"Why not?"

"It's hard work."

"I know." Jason flexed his arms. "I'm up for it."

"How long you been thinking about asking me for a job?"

"Oh, for a while now. I knew I wasn't going to stay enlisted. One tour was all I signed up for. One tour was enough." Jason shrugged, his gaze dropping to the table top. "So I was trying to think about what I want to do."

"And you immediately thought of me?" I was rather flattered by that.

"Well, you were third or fourth on the list," he admitted.

"Oh."

"Don't get me wrong! I enjoy the outdoors and gardening and stuff like that. I was thinking about different places to apply. I don't want to be cooped inside a factory working some production line. I'm not sure I want to go back to a cashier job at the grocery store either."

I got up to pour myself another mug of coffee. And I thought about pouring some whiskey into it. "You looking for full time work or just a summer job?"

"I—I'm not sure."

I had to give him bonus points for honesty.

"Summer job at least...I might be tempted to stay longer if I enjoy it enough. And if you need the help, of course, come fall and winter."

"I can probably find enough work for helpers." I usually turned down some of the snow clearing jobs I was asked about—I couldn't handle them all on my own. "You know, Jason, you could probably do a lot better than just working for me."

He shrugged.

"You've got experience. The military training."

"Yeah."

I stared at him.

"Like I said, the problem is that I don't know what I want to do. I don't want to be a store clerk or some stock boy. I really want something which gets me outdoors."

"Remember that you said those words when it's pouring rain and you're outside in it all day." I'd made my mind up already. "All right...you can start on Monday, if that works for you."

"That's fine. Thanks, Mister Owens."

He gave me a big grin which made me feel warm and tingly inside. "And it's not '*Mister Owens*,' either," I told him. "Just call me *Scott*."

"All right." His grin got even bigger.

"Eight thirty. If you're not here, I'll leave without you."

"I'll be here, Scott. I won't be late."

"Okay then...bring a lunch with you. Plenty of water too. Do you have a cooler? There are no fridges around."

"Yeah, we've got a small portable one I can borrow."

What am I getting myself into? I had to wonder that. *Having him around all day for me to moon over? What am I thinking?* It had to be the hangover talking.

* * *

Of course, it started raining just before noon on Sunday, and it poured down torrentially for the rest of the day and all night as well.

I sat in my living room window for a while and stared out at the rain.

With nothing better to do, I headed to my office and tried to concentrate on the bookkeeping. It was mid-month and I had to send out billing invoices to my regular clients and make sure everyone was paid up.

A few clients were always late. And two of them would try any excuse not to pay me. I'd already told James Ross that I was not going to do any further work on his property until he paid me what he owed from March and April. I'd be lucky to see that money—he had been blacklisted by three other landscapers for failing to pay his bills.

If I added him to that list, I doubt there'd be a single place in town that he could hire to look after his yard.

And he was probably one of the richest men in town.

I could only shake my head. The rich get richer, the poor stay poor, and those of us in the middle were caught in the middle and struggling to stay afloat.

I wondered if Jason would last all summer. I'd hired a helper last year—he'd quit after a month cause the sun was too hot for him. Hello, we're landscapers...we work outside!

Closing my spreadsheets, I called up the government website to download the forms I'd need for my new worker. Payroll, deductions, workman's comp...so much fucking paperwork. I grunted out a curse as the printer failed to work—it had a jam I had to clear.

It was only mid-afternoon and I needed a stiff drink.

Chapter Five

The doorbell rang and I opened it.

Jason was waiting on the porch. "Morning, boss," he said. He had his usual grin on his face, as if he was amused by something I'd missed.

"Morning, Jason." I gave him a matching smile. "You ready for the day's big adventure?"

"Yep." He nodded. He was wearing a unbutton, long-sleeved green shirt over a plain navy blue tee-shirt, blue denim shorts, and a pair of black *Nikes*. He had a small portable cooler on the porch beside him. "Am I dressed okay?" he asked.

I nodded again. "You look fine." *Those shorts really show off your legs.* He had really nicely shaped legs, with a coating of fine hair. *No wonder I missed seeing the hair last night.* I wondered how it would feel to run my hands up and down those legs...and I hastily shook away the thought.

"I figured layering would be smart right now. It's still a bit cool, but I'm sure it'll be hotter later."

"You'll definitely work up a sweat," I told him.

"Good...I'm not looking for an easy ride. I expect you to treat me like any other employee."

"I'll do that." I glanced at my watch. "We should get going." I returned to the kitchen to grab my own cooler, then I scooped up my truck keys and cell phone from the table.

Jason was still waiting out on the porch. "Do I get to drive?" he asked.

"Maybe." I certainly wasn't going to let him back up though. Not my trailer into my garage...it wasn't as easy as it looked.

* * *

The kid learned fast.

But then, we were only cutting grass. It didn't take much training to mow a lawn and then rake up afterwards.

I watched Jason sweep the driveway clean while I checked off an invoice and slipped it into the mailbox.

"Where too next?" he asked me as he put the broom into the trailer.

I checked the tarp holding the grass in place—he had already tied it down. "Marriott's next."

"Okay."

"Don't worry about the names," I told him as he reached for his cooler. "I have a pretty sizable client list right now, but you tend to go to the same places week after week. You'll learn the circuit quickly enough."

Jason popped open the tab on his *Coke* and took a long swallow. "Sounds good to me. So, did you always want to be a landscaper?"

"I wanted to be a cop," I told him.

"So what changed?"

"What kid really sticks with his daydreams? I changed my mind all right time. 'What do you want to be when you grow up?' Cop. Fireman. Cowboy. Movie star. I worked my way through just about everything before getting out of high school."

"And after college you ended up cutting lawns?"

"It's honest work." I chuckled. "More honest than most, and I enjoy it. I decided long ago that I was only going to work at something I enjoyed. I'm not looking to get rich, just earn a decent living."

Jason glanced at the pick-up and trailer. "I think you're managing it pretty well."

"Yeah, me too." I chuckled. "Of course, once the winter hits and the temperature drops, then you might change your mind. Shoveling snow when it's twenty below out isn't as much fun as soaking up the sun."

"I missed the snow and winter weather. Does that surprise you?" Jason took another sip of his *Coke*. "The desert was just hot sand. White, kinda like snow, but too hot. Way too hot."

"It's taken a long time to build up my business to this point." I shrugged. "A real long time."

I was still working hard to build up my fledgling business, and was relying heavily on relatives and neighbors to find enough customers. Landscaping—all right, lawn mowing—was still a part-time job. I hoped to earn enough money from it to pay off my last year of college, saving me from having to take out any student loans. It would also serve to keep me in shape. I hated going to a gym to work out on the machines—I found that to be a waste of time—but I would happily spend all day outside working myself into exhaustion.

Tyler, one of my buddies, was doing some serious landscaping on his yard. I'd volunteered to go over to his place and help him out. He jumped at the offer too—he had a black thumb, but wanted to have some colour in his yard to make his new wife happy.

"I'm sorry about how this place looks," Tyler apologized to me when I arrived at his place on my bike. We headed around the bungalow to the backyard.

"It looks fine to me," I replied.

"All that rain really made a mess of things."

By that point, we'd had nearly a week of rain. Good torrential showers and thunderstorms. The ground was pretty much entirely a wet and muddy mess.

"It's going to be perfect for gardening," I told him with a sloppy grin on my face. "Make it easy to dig in."

"Gonna be real messy."

I shrugged. "So what?"

"Just wanted to warn you."

"I'm ready for it." I had taken care to dress in my fun clothes—a green and blue stripped tee-shirt and faded blue *Wranglers,* with black *Action Basics* running shoes on my feet. Nothing too fancy, nothing I was really worried about keeping clean. It was all about comfort. Just looking at all the muddy ground made my dick hard in my purple silk boxer shorts. Tyler had no idea how much I actually enjoyed playing in the mud, so I was really looking forward to this. Still grinning in anticipation, I adjusted my tan ball cap.

Tyler looked at me, then at the yard, and he shrugged. He was wearing tight black *Levis,* a blue *Old Navy* tee-shirt, and gray running shoes.

I'd always liked hanging out with Tyler. Our personalities meshed really well. Same taste in comedy, same tastes in trashy movies, same enjoyment in a night playing war games. And Tyler's looks were a bonus.

He was hot...no, he was gorgeous.

He had a preference for almost always wearing tight jeans and tee-shirts and he had the body to carry them off. Tyler had a slender runner's build, beautiful blue eyes, short brown hair and goatee. He knew I was gay and I was sure that he dressed like he did just to torment me.

Anyway, I was going to enjoy today.

The wife was away.

The yard was a muddy mess.

It was going to be a good day.

Tyler had already planted some shrubs along the back fence—yews and cedars mostly. He wanted to put in a vegetable garden so I'd come over to help him work on that particular job.

A few hours of working with pitchforks and shovels and we had the grass torn up and exposed the dirt in a large rectangle. Needless to say, we were both getting pretty filthy by then. Between stomping through the muck and the like, my jeans had turned brown well past the knees.

I'd also been wiping my hands off on my thighs and tee-shirt so most of me was the colour of mud. And I was loving every second.

Tyler's denim-clad legs were also mucky—he'd been kneeling while planting the last of his shrubs, but that was mainly on the wet grass, not in the mud like me. Plus the denim of his jeans made it not as noticeable.

I was smiling as I stood up.

Tyler wiped his forehead. "This is harder than I expected."

"Wimp." I grinned at him. "don't be such a girl. We're just getting started after all. Lots more work ahead of us."

Tyler groaned. "Dig more holes for planting, right?"

"We still have to prep the ground before we do any planting." I was using a pitchfork, by then, to turn over the future veggie patch. We'd added peat moss and compost to the soil, trying to make it richer. It was a dark colour now and just as wet as the rest of the yard. Rather soupy.

"You are a mess!" he announced.

I just shrugged. "Oh well."

Tyler was shaking his head.

"My granny always told me that gardening is like sex," I told him with a big grin. "If you're still clean when you're done, then you did it all wrong."

"Well, Scott, you must be doing it right then. You've pretty much wrecked your clothes."

"They'll wash out."

Tyler turned towards his house. "I need a cold drink. You want one?"

"Yeah. Thanks."

Tyler set off towards the back porch. He splashed through a standing puddle, not taking the time to go around it.

I chuckled. This supposed 'buddy, I need a favour' was turning into heaven. A cute guy and lots of mud. And he thought I'd be hating this.

After a few minutes, Tyler stepped back outside, slipped his sneakers back onto his feet, and then walked over to me with a beer in each hand.

I wiped my hands off on my jeans again—it wasn't really doing much good by that point—and accepted the beer. It tasted real good.

Tyler was looking at the garden and shaking his head. "So now what?"

"We finish mixing this in and then we can start planting." I looked at him, a grin playing across my face. "You have all your plants right? Otherwise, we'll be going to the garden centre to buy some."

"Yeah, I got some over there." He waved his hand towards the shed.

Damn, I thought. *It would've been fun to go shopping while wet and muddy like this.* We'd get some odd looks from people, but it was a garden centre so *some* dirt had to be expected.

I could see the flats of plants Tyler had bought. "Looks like a good selection." I walked over to check on them. A fairly good assortment of basic vegetables.

"I didn't know what would grow best in the soil so I thought I'd try a bit of everything."

"That certainly works. Plant something of everything this year and see what thrives. Then you'll know better for next year." I looked back at the garden where we were working. "You might want to lay some flat stones in here as a path. That way you can get to your plants without having to wade through mud all the time."

"I was thinking about doing something like that. Liane gets bitchy whenever I track mud through the house. If we're going to be picking fresh produce and carting it inside...."

Liane is bitchy about everything *anyone does,* I thought. She didn't like me—I was afraid she thought I was after her husband. *Well, I am, but it's not like I'm going to ever catch him.* He loved her...for whatever reason.

I finished my beer and set the bottle down in the grass. "So if we want to get this over with, then we should get back to work. If we start digging the holes out here—" I waded out into the garden as I said that.

The mud was so nice deep by now. I sank down well past my ankles getting my running shoes, socks, and the cuffs of my jeans completely wet and muddy. I wondered if I should accidentally slip and fall. Just to get completely messed up. How often would I have this chance?

Tyler was shaking his head again. "You have mud on your ass," he told me.

"So what?" I replied as I turned to face him. Well, *tried* to turn. I really was semi-stuck now, my feet submerged in the thick muck. "It'll all wash off." I kept trying to turn around. "Damn," I swore. "I'm stuck."

Tyler laughed. "I warned you."

I gave my right foot a yank, sharper than I needed too, and that was all it took.

I fell over.

Tyler was laughing so hard that he dropped his empty beer bottle onto the lawn. There I was sitting in the garden patch, up to my waist in mud. I could feel the wetness penetrating through my jeans into my silk boxers. It made my dick twitch.

Tyler was hysterical with laughter. Finally he staggered towards me. "Yep," he wheezed, "all that mud will just wash off."

I stood up. Carefully. My jeans were heavier than they'd been. I looked down at them, pretending to be concerned. The blue denim was thoroughly coated with dark brown mud. They, and my tee-shirt, were now clinging to me.

"Damn, Scott, you really do get into this whole gardening thing."

I splashed my way through the mud towards him. "Yeah, yeah. Every one's a comedian." I held out my hand. "Steady me. I'm gonna loose a shoe in this."

Obediently, Tyler reached out to me.

And I grabbed his hand and threw myself backwards, pulling him off-balance.

He hit the mud with a nice splat. Face first, too. He was laughing though, so I knew he was okay with this surprise. If not, who cared? Tyler lifted his head to look at me, mud slowly dripping from his face. "You do realize, this means war?" he said in his best *Marvin the Martian* imitation.

"I do."

"Good." Tyler shoved me onto my back.

We wrestled, grappling with one another, and rolling around in the muck until we were both exhausted and totally plastered. Our clothes were identical now—brown.

Tyler sat up and tried to crawl away.

"Not so fast, big boy." I snatched my ball cap up, taking care to scoop mud into it, and then I plopped it down onto my head.

Tyler was still laughing. "You are crazy."

"I know." I grabbed at him again. "Get back here." My hands slid along his muddy jeans, brushing across his crotch.

Tyler froze.

So did I...he was sporting one serious hard-on.

Of course, so was I by this point and my mud-soaked jeans did nothing to hide it. The wet denim seemed to enhance the bulge. I decided to be a bit bolder. I slid my hands along Tyler's legs and groped him. Quite openly.

Tyler didn't move. He just sat there while I played with his tenting jeans.

"I can stop," I told him.

"You don't have to on my account."

That was enough of a reply for me. I quickly fumbled open his fly and reached inside. My muddy hand found nothing but warm skin. *"Commando...*you naughty boy."

"Dirty boy," he replied. He had taken a firm grip on my shoulders now. "You've made a nice mess of things here."

"I didn't hear you complaining," I countered.

We shifted positions, getting ourselves more comfortable.

"You want some help with this?" I asked him. I was still holding his dick, fondling the shaft.

"Sure," he replied.

I pulled him through the open zipper, taking a good look at his hard member, and then I quickly scooped up more mud in my hand and rubbed him with it.

Tyler gasped.

"Feels really good, doesn't it?" I laughed softly.

Tyler gasped again as I rubbed him. His hands were fumbling my own *Wranglers* open, allowing my own hard-on to escape from its silky confines.

"I never figured you for a boxers guy," Tyler said. "Let alone silk ones."

"Live and learn." They were something I'd started wearing after borrowing a pair from Alec on more than one occasion.

I reached over and began stroking him.

If anything, he seemed to get even harder.

Tyler cried out as he came.

A heavy stream of cum erupted from the end of his cock and splattered across the front of his jeans.

He grabbed my own shaft even harder and stroked more furiously.

"Oh, God, yes!" I gasped as I came.

We both collapsed, lifelessly, into the mud, panting.

After what seemed like hours, I finally mustered the energy to lift my head and look down at myself and then over at Tyler. We were both flaccid by then, with our jeans hanging open. His cum was sharply white against the dark brown mud which covered the black denim.

"So...you got a hose?" I finally asked.

I finished backing the trailer and pick-up into the garage. "Well, you made it through the first day."

Jason opened the door and climbed out onto the driveway. "I'll see you tomorrow."

"Looking forward to it." I watched him walk back towards his house. The way in which the fabric of his shorts clung to his ass as he walked made my own dick twitch. *I need a long shower,* I thought to myself. *A very long and very cold shower.*

There was a lot jerking off in the shower that evening. Hell, for just that whole entire week. I swear, I went through an entire bottle of baby oil in just that first week.

Working around Jason all day was giving me a near constant hard-on. It was worse than being room-mates with his uncle Alec!

Chapter Six

The first week came to an end and that Friday night I dropped Jason off at his place and then backed into my driveway. I headed inside my house, tossed the day's mail onto the table—the bills could wait until later—and then I headed to the bathroom and took a cold shower. It felt so good to strip off my jeans and tee-shirt and just stand under the water. I was trying to wash away the thoughts I was having about Jason.

It was a slow and subtle torture working around him day after day. Watching the manner in which his clothes clung to his body as he moved, to watch his muscular legs as he pushed the mower, or to catch a brief glimpse of his stomach when his tee-shirt rode up when he lifted things.

Just like being around his uncle....

I barely saw Alec for most of the week after our unusual threesome with Jeremy. We'd showered together, after the threesome, and then he helped me change my bedding—the cum-soaked sheets definitely needed washing—before retiring to his own bed to sleep Saturday night. He was out when I woke up that Sunday morning, and usually gone before I woke up during the week. I saw him in passing in a few of the classes we shared, but otherwise I was certain that he was deliberately avoiding me.

It was the following Thursday before I saw and actually spoke to him. He was in the kitchen, a glass of cola in his hand, looking tired and a bit ragged. His red tee-shirt was wrinkled and stained and his jeans didn't look much better.

"What's the problem?" I asked. *You've really let yourself go.* From the few times I'd seen him around the campus, he'd been wearing that same outfit all week. I was only dressed in a pair of snug boxer briefs, as had become usual. *We'd had sex twice now...what was the point of hiding our bodies from each other? We'd already seen everything.*

He looked at me and then shrugged. "Nothing." His eyes rested momentarily on my crotch, then he looked away. His cheeks were red.

"Liar."

"Nothing is wrong."

"Something is up, Alec. You've been avoiding me all week."

"I thought you'd prefer that. I mean, after you and Jeremy—"

"I thought you wanted that?"

"I did!" he replied defensively. He was swaying slightly.

"You don't sound like you did."

"Well..." Alec grimaced.

I could smell his drink from where I stood. It was a strong rum-and-*Coke*. Very strong. "Alec?"

"It's just Jeremy...he's more demanding lately."

"Are you and he a couple?" I asked. *Had I messed up a relationship?*

"No, not really. We just meet up to fool around." He looked somewhat embarrassed admitting that. "No strings. It's just sex."

"Oh."

"But..." His voice trailed off and he took a drink from his glass.

I was looking at him more closely. The tired eyes and raggedness, along with the gentle swaying, told me enough. "How much have you had to drink?"

"Not enough."

I moved closer. "I'm here if you want to talk."

"It's nothing, Scott."

"Alec, we need to talk about the other day."

"There's nothing to talk about." He downed his drink and immediately poured himself another one—there as much rum as cola in his glass. "Nothing important." He moved away from me, heading into the living room. "We broke up. Okay? Happy now?"

I followed him. "Alec...."

He had plopped down on the couch. "He was nice to me when we first got together. We'd meet and talk a bit, before having sex. Sometimes we'd go out and grab some pizza or something first. But he's changed." He was staring into his glass. "He wasn't always so demanding, so bossy." He took a compulsive swallow of his drink. "So mean."

He looked at me as I sat down next to him. "We had a meeting on Sunday and he wanted me to entertain a few of his buddies. I did, trying to make him happy, but he told me I wasn't putting my heart into it."

I winced.

"So I told him to fuck off. Told him to find another guy to boss around."

"You can do better than him," I agreed. "You don't need to be bossed around like that."

"No, I don't."

"Alec, you're a great guy. I couldn't have asked for a better roomie. Study partner. Friend even." I patted his arm. "I'm here for you, buddy."

He blinked his watery eyes.

That was good enough for me. I rested my hand on his knee, and when he didn't even glance down at it, I slowly ran it up his thigh until I encountered his bulging crotch.

He had a semi hard-on in his jeans and that startled me.

He didn't even twitch.

"Alec, I'm here for you." I was playing with his cock through his jeans as I spoke soothingly. "You can talk to me. I don't want you to think I don't care." I was still stroking him. "I want you to be happy." He was definitely getting harder. "I can stop if you want me too."

"No." He still wasn't looking at me.

I had my own hard-on now. The cotton boxer briefs were straining...and they didn't hide my arousal in the slightest.

Now Alec turned to me with a wild look in his eye. I expected him to say something, to tell me to stop, but he leaned slowly forward.

He wanted to kiss me...and I wanted it too. I leaned into it—he went overboard with his probing tongue, but the feel of his rough beard stubble against my cheeks and the way he put his hand behind my neck really made up for it.

Five minutes, ten, twenty? I don't know how long we sat there kissing.

At last Alec broke the kiss and sat back panting. "Fuck, you're hot. I've thought so since we first moved in together...."

"You should have spoken up."

"I didn't know you were into guys." He looked somewhat sheepish. "I didn't think you'd be into me."

I looked down at my crotch. "Do you think I'm lying?" I asked.

"Nope," he replied. He gave me a faint smile. "Do you want to carry this discussion into your bedroom?"

"Hell yes!" I replied. "But only if you're sure you want too."

"I do." He nodded. "I really do."

I stood up, and pulled him to his feet. "We can stop this any time," I reminded him. "Alec, I'm *not* Jeremy. I won't order you to do anything you don't—"

"You're talking too much!" He pulled me into his bedroom. "I've never had a guy in here." He started to pull at his clothes.

"Let me." He stood there, mouth hanging open, while I unbuckled his belt and then tenderly slid his jeans down his legs. He was bulging in his silk boxers—having crouched to remove his jeans, I paused to enjoy the view for a moment. Standing back up, I lifted his tee-shirt over his head and tossed it aside.

"You are cute," I told him. He wasn't overly muscular or built, but he was well-defined and lightly covered with reddish hair. And he had great eyes.

He seemed almost embarrassed being the object of my attention. He stood there, almost smiling but not quite, as I scrutinized him from every angle. Even his thighs and calves were hot, packed with muscle and exquisitely shaped and defined, with their light dustings of hair. A little exercise—maybe some jogging with me—and he would be even hotter.

I started working his nipples, teasing them lightly with my teeth and tongue until they grew hard. I continued to caress and pinch them with my hands as I kissed my way down across his stomach to the waistband of his boxers. I could see his cock outlined by the thin silk, and as I pulled the elastic band back, his dick sprang up to hit his stomach with a meaty slap. Grinning, I wrapped my hand around it, loving the hardness and smoothness of it. I slid my tongue across the head, which made Alec hiss with pleasure; I lapped at it a few more times, and then took it into my mouth.

"Damn, you really know how to work that tongue."

I managed a grin. I suspected that he was just unused to being the one getting head. I pushed him gently backwards until he fell into bed.

As soon as he was lying down, I redoubled my efforts, choking down his entire shaft until my nose was planted in his pubes. He tossed his head back and forth on the pillow, and moaned aloud. I took this as approval, and sucked him even deeper and harder, to the point where I had to let him go just to catch my own breath.

"Oh, Scott," he groaned, "you're doing a great job."

I dragged my tongue across his balls a few times, before returning to take his shaft in my mouth once again. I started sucking away, expecting that he wouldn't take long for him to shoot his load.

"Come over here," he whispered urgently. "Take your clothes off and get in bed with me."

Given the fact that I was only wearing my underwear, stripping took only a few seconds and then I was hopped into bed with him.

Alec took me in his arms, and kissed me as passionately as he had in the living room. The two of us rolled around on top of the sheets, our bodies rubbing against each other. Dick-to-dick, cheek-to-cheek.

"You feel so good," he whispered. "Jeremy never liked to do this."

"I'm not Jeremy," I reminded him. "Tonight is all about you," I told him. "We're only doing what you want too."

"I want you to fuck me," he said. "But in your own way."

"Are you sure?" I was thinking back to our first fuck. Thinking back on, especially now after hearing about Jeremy, it was too much like a rape for my taste. "I don't want to hurt you."

"You aren't going to hurt me." He ground his pelvis against mine to make his point. "Fuck me, Scott."

"Only if you're—"

"Fuck me!"

"All right," I said.

He kissed me. "Everything's in my jeans. Jeremy always wanted me prepared."

I frowned. The more I heard, the less I liked Jeremy. I rolled over and reached for his jeans. A condom and a small bottle of lube were in his front pocket.

Alec was smiling in anticipation. He rolled over, showing me his broad back and perfect ass. He even thrust his ass up a little in the air, so that his cheeks were naturally parted for me.

I applied a generous squirt of lube to his hole and slid my finger inside him.

I worked him gently for a few moments, loosening him up, then I straddled his ass, holding my cock so I could rub the head up and down his crack. I squirted more lube on my dick as I rubbed him with it, until finally when I zeroed in on his hole and slid it in.

I didn't force myself inside him. Not this time. No, I took my time, stroking his sides and kissing his shoulders, until finally I managed to land all the way in, my balls nestled up to his.

"Ah," he practically purred

I kept working my cock in and out of his clutching hole. Damn, I loved the way it felt when I pulled all the way out and slid it back in again. "Let me know if it hurts."

"It feels great," he said. "It feels so good."

"Yeah?" I slid out of him, and grabbed his legs to turn him over. I spread his legs wide and popped it into him face to face, so that he could watch my cock slide in and out of his tight fuzzy hole. "How do you like it now?"

He stared down at my shaft, mesmerized by the sight and the sound of my hips hitting his round firm ass cheeks. I was really enjoying this slow and sensual fuck. No, it wasn't a sex-fuck, it was lovemaking.

Even with my slower pace, I couldn't avoid cumming forever. I was holding back, gritting my teeth, clamping down with my cock muscles like crazy to keep from cumming, but it was no use. With a strangled half-yell I buried my face against his chest and let loose with spurt after spurt of hot cum in his tight gripping ass. I could dimly hear him groaning encouragements and cheering me on, but it was unnecessary; nothing could have stopped me from blasting all of my load out in his ass once I started.

When it was over, and my vision was still blurry, I leaned down to take him in my mouth.

"Too late," he apologized. His own cum was pooled on his stomach. "I couldn't stop myself."

"No problem." I lapped his salty cream up anyway, making him sigh and giggle.

After he was clean, I snuggled up against him...and the next morning, he was still there.

* * *

"So, do you need me for the weekend?" Jason asked as we pulled into the driveway and I prepared to back the trailer up. We'd ended the day early—I hadn't had many jobs scheduled so we were done everything by two.

I shook my head. "No, I don't have any jobs scheduled. I have a yard to go and look at later today, but otherwise, nothing until Monday." Our second week had come to an end. Working with him was still torture, but I simply jerked off every morning before getting up and usually two or three times at night. A few times, I'd ducked into a bathroom stall during a break to jerk-off quickly.

"Oh, okay."

He sounded disappointed by that. I frowned at his attitude. "What's with the eagerness to work? You've been pushing yourself the last two weeks. You got paid today. Now you have the weekend to spend with your family."

"My folks aren't going to be home. They're off to Toronto for a concert."

"Oh. Then go party with your friends."

"I am going tonight."

"See...you get to relax. I get to paint my living room."

Jason looked at me. "You want a hand with that?"

"Don't you see enough of me during the week?" I asked, half-jokingly.

"I don't mind. I don't have anything else to do right now. I'd be happy to give you a hand, Scott."

I felt my dick twitch in my *Levi's* at that comment. *I'd love to give you a hand,* I thought to myself. "Only if you're sure you want too. It's not a job requirement to come and paint my house."

"I don't mind. I'm not a very good painter though," Jason warned me. "I don't think I've painted anything since high school art class."

"I'll have tarps down."

That night, I watched a car pull up across the street. Its horn honked.

Jason came out of his house and waved. He was wearing a snug black tee-shirt and shorts.

The other three guys in the car climbed out and began backslapping. They were all smiling broadly.

Jason has some good-looking buddies, I noted. I'd seen them up close at the barbeque. *I'd happily drag any of them into my bed*. Not that there was any chance of that happening.

They piled into the car and drove off with a squeal of tires.

Damned punks, I muttered. Yep, I was definitely getting old.

Chapter Seven

Morning rolled around and I enjoyed my usual two cups of coffee.

I had moved most of the furniture either into the centre of the living room, or out entirely. I had picked up some cheap drop cloths from the local *Home Depot* and laid them over everything. They were thin plastic, but sufficient for protecting the couch etc from stray paint splatters.

I was ready to start. No sign of my erstwhile helper, but I wasn't counting on him to show. Who'd want to waste his weekend stuck inside painting? *He's probably still sleeping off the party with his buddies.*

I finished my coffee and put the mug into the sink.

I guess I should get to it, I said, trying to mentally psych myself up for the job. It wasn't easy, but I knew it had to be done. I hated painting though. Always had done.

The doorbell rang.

"Come on in!" I shouted.

Jason stepped through the door. "Morning, Scott."

"Morning, Jason. I didn't think I'd see you today."

"I said I'd be here." Jason was dressed for the job in a ratty dark green tee-shirt and cut-off denim shorts. He hadn't shaved either, and the stubble on his face gave him a scruffy and sexy look.

Fuck me...he looks like a walking wet-dream. I was dressed in an old pair of ripped-up *Levis* and a stained red tee-shirt which was too short and ragged to be worn in public. "You look tired."

He shrugged. "Late night last night."

"Oh?"

"Some buddies called and wanted to celebrate my being back home. We were out bar-hopping 'til after midnight." Jason managed to give me a grin. "We might have gotten a bit carried away."

"No kidding." I remembered those wild nights out with my buddies. "You still want to paint?" I asked him. "I figured you'd be sleeping it off."

"I said I'd come over and help you. I'm ready."

"All right."

I waved at him to follow me. "You want anything before we start?"

"No, I already ate."

"I've got fresh coffee."

"I'm fine."

"All right then." I shrugged and pointed him at the paint trays. "Then get to it." I mimed cracking a whip towards him.

He hunched over like some movie hunchback and shuffled into the living room. "Yes, master," he wheezed. "Right away, master."

I laughed.

We started with the ceiling.

Turned out that we were both really bad painters—we ended up with more paint on ourselves than on the ceiling and walls. Our faces and chests were covered in white paint, and my jeans were also splashed.

Breaking for a cold drink, I managed not to laugh at the splatters of paint on Jason's face.

"What?" Jason asked.

"Huh?"

"You're staring...did I miss a spot?" He looked at the wall behind him.

"No, you did a fine job." Catching sight of myself in the hallway mirror, I could see the white splatters on my own face. I tried to wipe some of the paint away.

Jason saw me. "You look like someone blew a load in your face," he laughed.

I looked at him, startled.

His laughter trailed off. "That is..." His face had gone bright red. "I mean—"

"I heard you quite clearly the first time." I could feel the big goofy grin on my face. Anyway, he looked so cute with white paint splashed over his body like bizarre alien freckles. I'd spent most of the day with a major hard-on inside my jeans and hoping he wouldn't notice.

Jason was definitely red in the face.

"Do you want to stop and clean up?" I asked him. My own dick was hard, inside my jeans, and I would've welcomed a few minutes alone in the bathroom. *Just give me a few minutes to jerk-off and I'll be good.* Otherwise I might just have to drag Jason to my bedroom and fuck him senseless.

Jason shook his head. "Naw, we should just keep working. Get the whole job done."

"Okay."

We kept painting.

"Well, that's a good job done," I said. The last portions of wall had been painted, the corners cut in, and the trim edged. Now it was just a matter of waiting for it to dry so I could move things back into place.

We carried the paint trays and brushes down into the basement.

"I'll deal with these." Jason turned on the taps of the laundry sink and began to wash the brushes clean.

I went back upstairs to get the drop cloths. I walked down the hallway, letting my hand brush lightly against my crotch. My erection was back again getting harder. For one brief moment, I thought about going back downstairs and grabbing Jason and giving him a passionate kiss.

I gave my head a shake. *Not going to do that,* I told myself. *Be professional about this. You can't just jump the young man's bones.*

I went back downstairs.

Jason had just finished washing out the trays and he hooked them over the edge of the laundry tub. "Man, I'm feeling hungry." He stretched his arms out over his head. "How about you?"

"Yeah...I'm thinking of just throwing a few burgers on the barbeque. You want to stay for dinner?"

"I'm sure there's something in the fridge at home." He didn't sound very excited by that possibility.

A smile spread across my face. "I don't mind. Anyway, you earned it."

"All right, I'll stay." He down looked at his tee-shirt and arms. "I should head back home and clean up though. I'm a mess."

"I've got an idea on that. Come on with me."

I led Jason out into the backyard.

"What's the plan?" he asked.

I uncoiled the hose and turned on the tap.

Jason frowned. "Now hang on a minute!"

I gave him a big grin, and squeezed the trigger.

"Yee-ahh!" he shouted.

I laughed as he jumped and tried to run.

With the gate closed, there was nowhere he could go.

"Don't be such a big baby!" I said as I sprayed him. I made sure to track the hose nozzle so that the water soaked all of his clothes. I felt my dick twitching as I very deliberately aimed the hose at his crotch and gave it a good spray.

I was trying to see how the fabric clung to his dick when he took advantage of my distraction and charged at me.

Exploiting his advantage, he managed to wrestle the hose out of my hand and turned it on me. "Don't be such a big baby!" Jason laughed as he pushed the nozzle past my waistband and sent icy water pouring down the insides of my *Levi's*.

We were thoroughly soaked by now. Our jeans were sagging from the weight, showing a few inches of soaked underwear.

"Fine," I replied.

We pulled off our tee-shirts, so that we could scrub the paint off our chests and arms.

The front of my jeans were bulging—I was sporting a major hard-on, and the wet denim clung nicely to it—and I was able to see a similar lump in the front of Jason's shorts. He didn't seem upset or concerned by our obvious states of arousal.

Is he really turned on by this? I wondered. *Was I going to get to see Jason strip down to a pair of wet clinging briefs?*

"That was fun, Scott." Jason gave me a somewhat sheepish grin. "I haven't had a water fight like that in years."

I shrugged. "Sometimes you just want to be goofy."

"That definitely qualified," he replied.

"It did," I agreed. *Just like yesterday afternoon....*

Alec came out of his house holding a second beer. He hurried down the back steps and across his yard to the fence.

I was standing in his neighbor's yard. After dropping Jason off at home, I had driven across town to make a final inspection of the Larochelle yard in preparation for some major landscaping and pool renovations. Alec had stood on his side of the fence talking to me while we surveyed the muddy mess the recent rains had left.

"Here you go, Scott."

"Wait!" I called out as Alec vaulted himself over the fence.

"Why—" Alec began, but it was too late for him to stop.

He landed in the mud with a loud splash.

This whole side of the fence—which he had been unable to see from his side—was nothing but soupy brown mud. The plants there already torn out by the owners.

"Fuck." Alec was standing in a deep hole, the mud was well past his ankles and soaking his gray slacks.

"Shit, man," I said. "I should've warned you sooner."

"Yeah." Looking rather embarrassed, Alec tried to step out of the hole. As he lifted one foot free from the mud, he slipped backwards. "Oh shit!"

I had to laugh.

Cursing up a storm, Alec sat in mud higher than his waist. It totally covered his pants and made the bottom of his mauve dress shirt cling to his abs.

"Damn it!"

My laughter finally trailed into silence. "Are you okay?" I wiped tears from my eyes with my hand. "You look so ridiculous sitting there in your nice clothes. You've got mud on your face...like freckles."

Biting his tongue against more curses, Alec stood up. His gray pants were coated with brown mud. His shoes were just lumps, wet mud dripping from his pants onto them. He certainly didn't look like someone who worked in a bank.

"Are you okay?" I was starting to chuckle again.

"I'm fine."

"That's...good," I managed between laughs. "I'd hate...for you...to have hurt...yourself."

"I'm fine." Alec grinned and then lunged at me.

I was tackled before I even realised I was in danger.

On his knees, Alec managed to get me in a headlock. "You were laughing...how do you like it?"

"I guess this is fair." Then he shifted and knocked Alec off-balance.

The two of us rolled around in the warm mud. It was like cake batter or pudding, thick but still soft. We were plastered, but that wasn't good enough for Alec—he shoved handfuls of mud inside my tee-shirt and down the front of my jeans.

I was definitely aroused.

When we finally slumped apart, we were exhausted from the wrestling. We were both totally covered by muck. Our skin and clothes were completely brown in colour.

Alec was turned on by the wrestling—the front of his slacks bulging with an obvious hard-on.

My own jeans were tented too. I pushed Alec onto his back. "Did you like that? Did it get you all worked up, grappling with me like that?"

"You know it did," Alec replied. His dick was straining against his fly.

"It's been too long since we did anything like this," I told him. I was still pinning Alec in place. "Too long since you were properly used"

Alec stared at me.

I unzipped my fly and pulled out my dick. I was so hard.

Alec reached up with some mud and began to stroke me—it was just like that time with Tyler, which Alec knew nothing about. The mud was silky in texture, just like pudding.

All too soon, I grunted and shot my load onto Alec's face. It dripped onto his shirt.

"You've still got the magic touch." I stood up. "Like I said, it's been way too long." I finished zipping up my jeans, then reached down and pulled Alec to his feet.

Alec tried to brush some of the mud from his clothes. He was smiling though.

I was looking at the murky pool.

"You really are draining it, right?" Alec asked.

"Damn right I am." Draining it was the only way I could repair the cracks in it.

"Good."

Both of us took running dives into the water.

Alec surfaced and swam back towards the shallow end. The water was even more murky now. He stood there, waist-deep.

I swam up beside him. I stood up as well, my tee-shirt clinging to my broad chest. "That was awesome. You don't know how many times I've wanted to just jump into a client's pool after a sweaty day's work." I waded to the stairs and climbed out onto the deck. My formerly blue tee-shirt was still brown, and my jeans were a brownish blue, and all of my clothing clung to every curve of my muscular body.

Alec moved and I glanced down at him. His pants were still bulging with his hard-on. He reached underwater, obviously rubbing himself through his slacks.

"Let me." I dove back into the deep end of the pool. Staying submerged in the muddy water, I unzipped his pants and reached for his cock. Without coming back up for air, I took him into my mouth and within moments Alec shot his load.

I surfaced, a big smirk on my face. "Feel better?"

"Hell, yeah."

I waded back towards the steps. "I wish I could stay here longer and play some more."

"But you've got to go?" Alec reluctantly followed after me.

"Yeah. Dinner date with friends."

"Damn." Alec climbed up the steps and onto the deck. His still-dirty dress clothes were clinging tightly to his body. I doubt that suit would survive.

"Like I said, I wish I could stay and play." I gave him a wink. "But I will be here all week working in the gardens."

"With your crew?"

"They'll leave at five...I can linger around here doing odd chores until you get home from the bank." I was eying Alec openly, clearly enjoying the sight of the other man's body through his clinging shirt and pants. "You're off at five, right?"

"I'm *done* at five...I suspect I'll be off about five thirty."
I had to laugh.

Chapter Eight

Monday morning rolled around and Jason was at the truck waiting for me.

It remained torture to work with him.

Staring at his hunky body day after day. Watching the material of his shorts and shirt riding on his body when he bent or lifted things. The near constant grin on his face—he had it every single time he looked at me.

It was torture to me. I had a near-constant hard-on in my jeans during the day. And that was after furiously jerking off every morning before going to my truck.

It was like being around his uncle...

* * *

"Hey, Alec, I just wanted to stop by for a moment. I've got my partner working on the last few plants now."

Alec Carmichael was standing inside the doorway of his house. He was still wearing the same gray suit which he had worn to work that day. "You're working my nephew hard?"

"Yeah." I narrowed my eyes—his pants still had a slight brownish tinge to them. *They must be the ones he was wearing two Fridays ago, I thought, when he hopped across the fence and slipped in the mud. I* didn't think it was the same shirt though. *That mauve shirt was beyond salvaging.*

Alec glanced towards the neighbor's house.

I followed his gaze. Jason was out of sight, working in the back.

"That job didn't take you long."

I shrugged. Two weeks...and this was only the second time I'd been here working when Alec was actually at home. "You can tell Jean-Marc and Claude just how efficient I am."

"I will." Alec was looking at me, his eyes travelling up and down my body.

I flexed slightly. My jeans and tee-shirt were worn and dirty from the day's work in the garden, but I knew that would help to make him even hornier. *Is that a bulge in his slacks?* I thought it was.

"So what brought you over here?"

"I wanted to thank you for recommending me to do the job."

"It was nothing. They've been talking about redoing the garden and pool for years. I just mentioned your name to spur them into action." He gave me a smile. "They like hiring hunky guys for any jobs."

I couldn't help but smile at that.

"I mean, I've known them to call and order a pizza...and they request 'the cutest delivery boy you have'. God, there must be a bunch of traumatized pizza delivery boys in town."

"Speaking of eating...I was thinking that we should go out for dinner."

Alec frowned. "Dinner?"

"Yeah...why not? We haven't gotten together in ages." Our backyard mud wrestling match and mutual jerk-off session from a week ago not withstanding. I briefly wondered if I should take him back into the neighbor's yard and have my way with him again. *That would give Jason a sight he'd not soon forget*! "When was the last time we had dinner? Or caught a movie?"

"Are you asking me out on a date?"

"Of course not. It's just dinner with a friend."

Alec was looking a bit sheepish. "I'm seeing someone. Sort of."

"Oh, really?"

"Yes, really."

"This seems sudden."

"It's not. Okay, it is. Sort of. It's complicated."

I laughed. "I'll take your word for it." I paused, looking at him. "So...dinner Friday night?"

"All right." Alec licked his lips. "Where do you want to go?"

"Somewhere nice. Maybe we should dress up...I was thinking about *Paulo's Trattoria*."

"You're going to dress up too?" He was licking his lips quite openly now. "You always cleaned up so nice. And it's so rare to see you in a suit."

"Thanks." I gave Alec a smile, then shook my head. "I do dress up on occasion." I owned one black suit. "I should get back to helping Jason with the yews. I'll see you Friday night. Sixish good for you?"

"Yes, that's good." Alec frowned. "Are you still going be working at Jean-Marc's on Friday?"

"Yeah, should be just done it by then."

"Well, it seems silly for you to drive all the way back across town to your place to clean up and change to come back here. Why don't you just bring your suit with you and you can shower and change here?"

"All right." I turned to leave. "Thanks."

* * *

Friday rolled around and we were finally done the Larochelle gardens and pool. It had been a bigger job than I had first planned. I figured they'd be happy with the job when they came home from their trip.

Walking around their house, I gave Jason the keys to the pick-up truck. "The lawns for the Jeffersons, the Ardens, and the Marriotts need mowing and this job is just about done." I had given him three addresses with grass to cut. "I'm trusting you to do a good job without me."

"I can do it," he replied with a grin. "No problem."

"Good. I want to make some last alterations and touch-ups here." The cleaned and refilled pool was sparkling. The gardens looked good, but the new gate on the fence still needed painting. I was waiting to see how the pool motor sounded as well.

"I'll come back tonight to get you," Jason said.

"Don't bother," I replied. "I'm going out for dinner with your uncle."

"Oh."

Why did he look so disappointed? "That means you get to back this monster up. Don't scratch the trailer or my garage."

"I won't."

I trusted him. I had too.

"How will you get home if I have your truck?"

"I'll take a taxi home tonight." I reached into the back of the truck cab and pulled out the sports duffle bag I'd packed in there earlier. "See you Monday morning."

"If not before," he replied.

* * *

I closed the bathroom door with a loud click. I was half surprised that Alec hadn't followed me into the shower. *He certainly looked liked he want to follow me in here.* Why was he restraining himself? *Does he really have a boyfriend?* It was certainly possible.

I stripped off my sweaty tee-shirt, then unzipped my jean shorts. Stepping out them, I looked at myself in front of the mirror. I had shaved that morning so I looked fine—or at least, I would once I washed the day's grime and sweat away.

The shower was nice and relaxing. I helped myself to Alec's body wash and shampoo. I wanted to smell good.

After towelling myself dry, I got dressed for our dinner-date. Black suit jacket and slacks, cream-coloured shirt, navy blue tie. I only owned one suit—I generally only dressed up for funerals and weddings. The rest of the time, it was either jeans and a tee-shirt, or a polo shirt and slacks if I needed something dressier.

I finished knotting my tie, then opened the bathroom door and stepped out into the hallway.

Alec was standing in the hallway. "You ready to go?"

"Yep."

Alec had changed out of the suit he'd be wearing when he answered the front door. That one had been brown. Now he was dressed in a gray suit—the same one he'd been wearing when we had our mud wrestling match. The jacket tapered down from his broad shoulders to his slim waist and then flared out just a bit, to cover his crotch and butt. He had a mauve-coloured shirt under the jacket, along with a yellow silk tie.

"Well?" he asked.

"Well?"

"You're undressing me with your eyes...do I pass muster?"

"Of course...how about me?"

"Oh yeah." He nodded. "You are one hot stud, Scott. You look good no matter what you wear."

"Even in my dirty work tee and jeans?"

"Even then."

I gave him a grin.

We had walked from his place to the restaurant. It was a nice night for it. It was only a few blocks away as well, hardly far at all.

The restaurant was one of the better ones in town. With the candles and low lighting, the entire night was turning out to be a romantic one. Not that I had planned on it begin one—we were just friends. Fuck-buddies. This was a no-strings attached meal. Which was almost disappointing given how good the meal actually was.

The entire evening was long and wonderful.

"This has been fun," Alec commented as we looked at each other across our empty plates and sipped at our wine.

I nodded. "Yeah." I took another drink from my wine glass, emptying it. "You want dessert?"

"I shouldn't."

"But you're going too...."

"Yeah."

I couldn't help but grin. Alec's sweet tooth was still there.

Chapter Nine

I had thoroughly enjoyed myself, and there was no question in my mind that Alec had as well. After our cake and coffee, we walked slowly back to Alec's house. The sun had set by now, but the late June night was still warm enough to enjoy. We had nothing to rush back for and just enjoyed our after dinner stroll and some quiet conversation. Neither of us was dressed for a jog anyway.

Alec unlocked his front door and we stepped inside the foyer. He clicked on the wall-mounted light and then tossed his keys onto the small console table.

I followed him into the living room where he clicked on a stand-lamp.

"It's been too long since we've had a chance to get together," Alec commented. He sat down on the leather couch.

I sat down beside him. "Yeah, it has."

"And how long will it be before I see you again? With the yard done, you won't be coming around here anymore."

"You have my cell."

"Yeah. You have mine too."

That was true. I nodded, smiling somewhat ruefully. It was just too easy to put off calling my friend. *Which is why it's been months and months since we got together.* It wasn't always about sex. "You want to go and see the yard?"

"Yeah, I would." Alec started to empty out his pockets, tossing his cell phone and wallet onto the coffee table.

"What's up?" I asked.

"I don't want to lose anything outside," Alec replied. "It's pretty dark in the backyard by this time of night. I don't fancy trying to find my keys or cell phone by flashlight later on." He gave me a grin. "Unless you have a key to their house to turn on the back lights."

"I don't." I shook my head. "If they hid one outside, they never told me where it was."

"Then you might want to leave your phone here too. I'll leave my backdoor unlocked so we can get back in."

"Okay." I shrugged in agreement, then emptied my own pockets. I only had my wallet and cell phone with me. Jason had all my keys—but I hid one outside so I'd still be able to get back inside my house.

We headed outside. We were both still wearing our suit jackets. They weren't really needed, temperature-wise, but neither of us had thought to remove them.

I opened the gate and we stepped into the backyard. "Here it is," I said. There were a few solar-powered lights glowing along the fence and around the pool. Combined with the moon, there was just enough light to see.

Alec paused near the picnic table. There was a tikki torch stuck in the ground next to it. He fumbled with something and a spark lit the torch. "There we go," he announced happily. "Now we can actually see your work."

The torch smoked, but he was right. We could see a lot better now.

Alec walked at my side, leaning close to me as I pointed out the new shrubs and other landscaping features Jason and I had installed.

"And you got the pool all cleaned up."

"Yes." I'd had to drain it completely to repair some cracks—which was a good thing cause the recent torrential rains had flooded mud into it. The landscaping had knocked even more debris into the water. And Alec and I had jumped into the pool after our impromptu wrestling match a few weeks ago.

As Alec stood staring across the yard, I wandered over to the edge of pool and squatted down to dip the fingers of my left hand into the water.

"So how's the water?" Alec asked he joined me.

"It still feels cold. It will take a few days of hot sun to warm up enough to really enjoy it."

"I don't know about that. When it's too warm, it's like getting into a bathtub. I want it to be refreshing." He dipped his own fingers into the pool. "Yeah, this is more my taste."

"Yeah?"

Alec had a grin on his face. "I love it cold like this."

"Should we go back to your place and get some trunks?"

"Not right now." Alec grabbed my hand and pulled me to my feet. He wrapped his arms around my waist and pulled me towards him. We stood face-to-face for a moment, and then he moved his head forward.

We kissed. It was deep and slow, our lips locked as our tongues gently probed each other's mouths.

Finally we broke apart.

"I've missed that," Alec said. "Why don't we ever stay together?"

I shrugged. "I don't know." For a moment, I saw Jason's face instead of Alec's. "We've always had great sex."

"True. But we drift in and out of contact. We need…damn, I don't know. Something."

"Yeah." I frowned at him. "I thought you were seeing someone?"

"I am…sort of. Maybe you and I should stop these get-togethers. Just be friends, not fuck-buddies."

"You really think that?"

"I think you get my blood boiling when I see you." Alec smiled at me as he slowly unwrapped his arms from my waist and placed them on my shoulders. "Maybe we should cool off."

I frowned, but then found myself falling backwards as he gave me a shove.

The pool was cold and the splash was loud as I made a very ungraceful dive.

I surfaced, spluttering and coughing. "What the fuck?" I gasped. I was treading water in the deep end of the swimming pool. It was an unusual feeling—I was used to getting soaked in jeans and tee-shirts, not a suit.

Alec was standing on the deck, still dry, and grinning widely.

I thought about splashing him.

"So, you feel cooled off?"

"Why not come in and see for yourself?" I countered. I wasn't really upset with him. Surprised, yes, but certainly not upset. If anything, I was amused that he had pulled off this prank. *I see why you had us empty our pockets,* I thought.

"Well...."

He was close enough to grab. I reached out and took a firm grip on his leg, pulling him off-balance so that he fell into the water with me.

He resurfaced, his hair plastered against his head, the same as mine was. He swam to my side and started treading water. He was still grinning, his amusement plain on his face.

"You're crazy, you know that?"

"Yeah," he replied. "And you love it."

"You wrecked my suit."

"It'll dry out. You're totally turned on by this. Admit it."

I felt myself cheeks getting hot—his hand brushed against my crotch and I knew he could feel my erection. The feeling of the water pushing my slacks against my skin

was erotic. There was simply no other word for it. The heaviness of the soaked shirt and jacket was oddly comforting. It reminded me of how I felt when I was laying in someone's arms. Like Alec's.

He was still looking at me.

"I'd rather do this naked."

He laughed. "Jean-Marc and Claude are always inviting me to join them here for some late night skinny-dipping. They'll be sorry to find out they missed it when I finally broke down and did."

"Come on." I swam towards the shallow end of the steps.

Alec followed me.

We stood on the deck in our dripping wet suits and ties. The tikki torch was flickering brightly. The air felt a lot cooler now than it had when we were dry.

"So, are we going back in?" I asked.

"Yeah."

"Then we should get these clothes off."

"Yep." Alec walked towards me.

I reached for my sodden tie to loosen it.

"Let me."

I smiled, feeling my dick twitch. Getting undressed by another guy was always fun and Alec had stripped me enough times that I knew just how enjoyable this was going to be.

We might not even get back into the pool...we'd likely end up having sex right here in the grass.

Alec reached out and gently placed his hand on the front of my jacket. "You make me crazy," he said. With that, he gripped my pocket firmly and yanked down.

I stumbled forward a step, caught by surprise.

Alec yanked again and this time we both heard the sound of ripping fabric.

I looked down at the tear in my jacket. "What the—"

"I said, 'you make me crazy'."

As he yanked a third time, tearing my other pocket free, I was stunned. *What was getting into him?* I closed my half-open mouth as Alec let the strips of material hang loosely beside my legs.

Now he laughed. He stood with his arms crossed on his chest and laughed.

"What the fuck are you doing?" I demanded. "This was my only suit."

"I just wanted to try something new."

"Oh, all right then." I nodded my head. "So then you won't mind if I return the favour?" With that, I reached out and firmly grabbed the lower pockets of his jacket and yanked. Hard.

The sound of ripping cloth made my dick twitch and it also sent a surge of joyful vengeance through me. I knew the banker had lots of suits, unlike me, but I was caught up in the spirit of the moment.

"Happy now?"

"Yes." Alec's suit jacket looked just like mine.

"Good. Then we can move to round two!" With that Alec grabbed me in a sudden bear hug and laid one hell of a kiss on my lips. My head swam at the unexpected passion of his kiss—and I could feel his hard-on pressing against my own crotch—until he broke off his kiss.

Alec was fumbling at my suit again, undoing the buttons and pulling my jacket open. He ripped the inner pockets apart, tearing the lining.

When he paused, I launched my own counterattack on his jacket, quickly rippling it apart to match my own. We were acting like kids.

Alec just stood there, while I pretended to be a tailor. I didn't stop either. As he stood looking at me and chuckling, I reached over and grabbed his left sleeve. I tugged at it, but the seams held. *Damn*! Giving up, I reached for the lapels and tugged at them.

The rags of Alec's soaked jacket fell to the deck.

I licked my lips. The mauve dress shirt clung wetly to Alec's chest and served to emphasize every muscle on his torso. Alec wasn't wearing an undershirt, for which I was thankful. His sodden gold tie, hanging down from his neck and ending just before his belt buckle, seemed to somehow add to the effect.

Alec didn't move while I paused to stare. I reached out and spun him around so I could see his back. His pants were dripping, the sodden suit material of his pants clung to his butt cheeks and in and around his crotch. The manner in which those soaked slacks clung to his ass was incredible. The light gray colour of the cloth had darkened almost to black. I stared, trying to take in every gorgeous inch.

"You look so fucking hot right now," I told him. I ran my hands over that amazing ass.

"Oh? You're not half-bad yourself."

I continued to caress that ass. Letting a grin twist my mouth, I let my fingers slide into those hip pockets...and then I tugged.

The right pocket tore down the left side and stopped when the pocket was hanging loosely. The right side of the right hip pocket refused to tear.

The left pocket tore easily and continued long past the end of the pocket. As I continued to pull down, the tear kept going well into the back of the left pant leg, which exposed not only Alec's leg, but also allowed me to see that he was wearing blue silk boxer shorts.

Now I took a firm grip on both sides of the tear and took a deep breath. I pulled my hands apart and the sound of ripping cloth filled the air as I finished destroying Alec's left pant leg. I spun him back around.

Alec handsome face was beaming with amusement. His smile showed me how much was enjoying this and how much he approved of my new tailoring.

From the front, Alec's partially ripped pants looked normal, aside from the bulging crotch. My own dick was rock-hard too. This whole rip-strip was a new experience for me...but I think I liked it. No, I know that I did—the act of literally ripping the clothing off of another guy was intensely arousing.

I hooked my left hand into the front pocket of his pants and pulled. I was almost startled by the sound of the side seam giving way. I tugged and pulled until I had torn those pants open all the way to the cuffs.

Of course, I had to repeat the manoeuvre on the other side, tearing that seam out as well.

Alec looked down at his tattered pants. We could both see his legs plainly through the holes. "I guess I won't be wearing these to work again," he commented.

"Nope." I reached down and undid his belt, taking the opportunity to grope his bulging crotch in the process. I pulled it out of its loops and tossed it aside.

"Are you just going to leave me like this?"

"Oh no." I stroked my fingers along his zipper. "I'm only just getting started." I grasped the material in my hands and pulled.

The zipper didn't give way.

For a moment, I thought I'd have to go and find a pair of scissors or a pocket knife.

Then the button gave way and material tore along side the zipper.

Alec's pants were well and truly ripped off.

And that revealed his silk boxer shorts and the hard dick trying to escape them. The boxers were still wet and clung suggestively to Alec's cock and balls, making it seem even larger.

I reached out to stroke that shaft, ever so gently.

Alec groaned and shuddered and for a moment, I thought he was going to shoot his load right there. He was still smiling, his eyes closed in ecstasy, while I played with his dick. "Fuck," he moaned softly.

"In due time," I replied. I stopping playing with him so I could loosen the knot of his tie. Then I ran my fingers along his chest, flicking his nipples through his shirt.

He groaned.

I ripped his dress shirt open, buttons flying into the grass.

"Fuck, yeah!" Alec was fumbling with me now, tearing my jacket completely off and following it with the pieces of my now-shredded shirt. He torn the pockets loose, the pulled the buttons open. His hands dropped down to fumble at the front of my black slacks. His dick was bouncing visibly inside his silk boxers. "Let's do it!" He yanked my zipper down, and pushed me into the grass so that he could pull my slacks off.

I reached up and tore the fly of his boxers open, finally freeing his cock.

He returned the favour, tearing my boxer briefs open, and climbing on top of me. My own dick was just as hard and already leaking.

My lips pressed against his, and our tongues probed deeply. My hand wrapped around Alec's rock-hard cock and stroked gently. He moaned softly—we were outside in a city backyard after all—while I kissed his neck and shoulders. My left hand squeezed his nipples again.

I broke off our kiss, rolling us over, so that I was on top and so that I could move down his body and take his cock into my mouth.

I swallowed it, taking in as much as possible without gagging. I managed to take the whole thing into my mouth, until my nose was pressed into his blond pubic hair. He smelled good. His cock tasted good too, clean and fresh, with just a hint of chlorine from the pool.

Alec's hips thrust upwards to meet my mouth.

I let my mouth glide over his cock gently making his body shudder. He was so obviously enjoying this whole session. *How much of this did he plan?* I had to wonder. *Was this a spur of the moment thing or did he always want to have this rip-strip session?*

"Hang on a minute." Alec shifted under me—I never stopped sucking on his shaft—until we were in a sixty-nine position. He took my balls into his mouth, and licked them, sending shivers through me.

"Mmm," I groaned, my mouth still full of his own cock.

Alec released my balls so that he could take my cock into his mouth. He really was good that—he had been a cock-sucking master in college.

I was so lost in the good feelings, I didn't even realize that he was getting close to blowing his load.

Then I tasted a spurt of pre-cum on my tongue, and I savoured the precious liquid for a moment before swallowing. I began to pay more attention to his cock, waiting for the pay-off.

Alec was still sucking my dick, and running his fingers lightly up and down my ass-crack. *Oh God!* I thought. He began to probe my hole. That felt really good and my moaning broadcast that clearly.

That sound was all Alec needed to hear. He slid his finger in, working it slowly in and out of my ass, mimicking how he was working my dick.

And how I was sucking on his. I could feel his cock getting harder, could tell he was close to shooting by how it was throbbing in my mouth. I prepared for the hot blast of cum.

"Uggh!" He moaned as loudly as he could.

My mouth filled with that warm, salty fluid. I swallowed and then grunted as I shot my own load into his mouth.

"Urg," Alec groaned as I collapsed onto the ground beside him. He shifted his body so that he was laying with his head on my chest.

We lay in the grass for what felt like hours, panting and trying to catch our breath.

"I can't believe we just did that." Alec finally sat up, looking down at me. His gold tie hung loosely down his chest.

I stared back at him. "You were an animal," I told him.

"Yeah...we both were." He half-stood. "That was amazing," he told me. "You were amazing." Now he squatted down, picking at the remains of our clothes in the darkness. The torch had run out of oil and guttered out. "Hmm."

"What?" I asked.

"We're going to have some fun heading home like this." He tossed my slacks to me, then wrapped his torn jacket around his waist. "Good thing it's just next door."

I laughed. "Now's a good time to think about that."

Chapter Ten

"So, you got big plans for the July first weekend?" Jason asked me as I turned the truck around a corner. The trailer rattled and clanked behind us.

"Nothing yet...likely just lounging around the house. Maybe go out to a bar or something that night." Not that the bar scene really interested me. Most of the guys there were just posers looking for a quick blow-job. "What about you?"

"We're thinking about going on a family camping trip."

"Oh." I gave him a smile. "So you want to book some time off?"

"Yes, boss." Jason nodded his head, that usual boyish smile on his face. "And Dad wanted to know if you felt like coming with us."

It was tempting. I always enjoyed camping—I'd gone with Mike and his family before, but not in the last three years. *Not since well before Jason left for boot camp.*

Jason was stretching out his arms. His tee-shirt was pulled tight across his chest, showing how filled out he had gotten.

I made myself look away. *Tempting, but did I really want to spend even more time around Jason?*

"You don't have to answer right away," Jason said. "You've got a couple of weeks to make up your mind."

"I'd love to go with you guys. It's been way too long since I was last camping." I had nothing better to do for that weekend after all.

* * *

We piled ourselves into Mike and Jessica's station wagon. I *volunteered* to sit in the backseat with Jason and Sarah—Jason let me have the window. It was a mistake on my part, as I spent most of the drive up the highway trying to hide a hard-on in my shorts while bumping legs with Jason. Luckily I hadn't tucked my tee-shirt into my shorts, so it just bunched up on my crotch, hiding most of my bulge.

Sneaking a few glances at Jason made me wonder if his own baggy tee-shirt was meant to be hiding his own arousal. The front of his shorts seemed to be bulging more than usual.

If he was gay, I'd swear he flirting with me. I'd had that thought before, but always dismissed it. *He's straight. It's just my imagination.*

To me, finally getting going that morning had seemed like it was taking forever. The last minute packing of the camping gear—I didn't own any to pack—and groceries—I bought a lot of our planned supplies as my contribution to the trip—and then the last minute decisions on where everyone was going to sit finally got resolved. I didn't bother arguing with anyone...this was their trip and I was just tagging along.

Stopping at the gas station, just up the road, was an eye opener. There was quite a line, even with the expected jacking up of the price.

"You can't tell me that the gas companies aren't in collusion," Mike grumbled as he swiped his credit card through the slot on the pump.

"You sure I can't pay for that?" I asked.

"No, Scott." Jessica shook her head. "You bought all those groceries."

"I just want to pay my fair share."

"Don't worry...you can work it off." Jessica chuckled, affecting a rather nasty accent as she laughed. "I like having shirtless men do my every bidding."

So do I, I thought to myself.

"There's an old pump and well back at the office," Jessica continued in her usual tone. "'You can be our water-boy."

Mike quickly nodded his own agreement. "It's just half a click away. Or so."

I remembered that well from a past visit. 'Half a click' as the crow flies maybe...what felt more like two kilometers up and down the dirt road. Not many shortcuts cross country either.

"It looks like just about everyone is leaving the city this weekend." Jason whistled. "I'd forgotten just how much traffic is around here."

"We'll be leaving it behind," Mike told him. "Just the four of us and empty forest."

* * *

Between the late start, the heavy traffic, Mike's back road *short-cut* getting us lost for a couple of hours, and the chatter with the campground owners at the office, we arrived at their preferred spot with just enough sunlight left to set up the tents. It really had been awhile since I'd last been camping so I had to read over the instructions to figure out how to set it up.

"I can help you get it up."

"What?"

Jason was watching me with a smile playing around his mouth. "The tent, I mean."

"You remember how to do this?"

"Yeah. We set up plenty of tents out in the desert."

"Those would have been different."

"A tent's a tent."

I nodded my head. "All right." We had three of them, all small, but sufficient for us to sleep in. *If it rains though, we're gonna go stir crazy.*

Jason looked over his shoulder. "Scott and I can share this one," he announced. "Guys only," he told his sister. "You can have the other tent all to yourself."

Sarah smiled happily. "Good...you snore."

Mike laughed at that. He and Jessica already had their tent mostly up.

"Mom just wanted to bring the two tents to start with," he told me as we worked on our own tent. "Dad and I overruled her. I said that Sarah would be happier if she was alone. Dad wants to be alone with mom." He gave a melodramatic shudder. "Ugh...my parents having sex."

I chuckled. I'd been camping once with Alec...tents were cramped places for two people having sex, but it could be done. *Keeping the other people nearby from hearing you, though, that was the* real *challenge.*

We finished getting the tent up.

Then we realized just how small that so-called two-man tent really was. We had to leave most of the extra gear in the station wagon in order for us to have enough room to actually sleep.

"See, Mom," Jason announced as we carried a duffle bag of extra clothes back to the wagon, "and you wanted to cram us into just two tents?"

Jessica sniffed loudly.

We did the traditional first night cooking. Hot dogs on sticks roasted over the open fire. There was something about that smoky flavor which just made them taste so good!

Then we sat around the campfire, drinking and talking. Loons were crying out on the lake. The moon and stars were bright—living in the city left us with the illusion of a nice sky...the reality in the country was so much brighter.

Sarah, of course, had straight cola but the rest of us added a little rum to our own cans to spike it.

Okay, some of us added more that just *a little*.

Sarah was the first to head to her tent and bed, but eventually Mike and Jessica also announced they were retiring. From the looks they were giving each other, I figured that the fresh air had done wonders to wake up their libidos.

An owl hooted.

The fire had reduced itself almost into smoldering embers.

Jason yawned. "You want me to toss another log on?" he asked.

"No, I'm thinking about turning in." I stifled a yawn of my own. "All this fresh air is too much for an old guy like me."

"Yeah right." Jason chuckled as he kicked dirt over the embers. "You spend all day out in the fresh air."

"Country air is different to city air," I pointed out. "It's a lot more tiring."

Jason eyed the dowsed campfire one more time, then sauntered towards the tent.

I followed after him. The moon gave me enough light to see...nothing in great detail, but more than just shadows and silhouettes.

Jason lit a small battery-operated lantern to give us some light inside the tent. "You can read for a bit if you want," he told me.

"No, I'm good."

Changing clothes was a real effort in the tent. We were both trying to undress at the same time, with not quite enough space for either of us to stand fully erect or move around without bumping into each other.

"Do you want me to wait outside?" I asked him. After all, did Jason really want me in the tent while he got undressed for bed? *What is he wearing to sleep in?* I wondered. I'd planned to just sleep in my boxers.

Jason already had his tee-shirt off. "Nah, I'm not shy." He was unfastening the drawstring on his nylon shorts. As he let them slip to the floor of the tent, I caught a glance of his designer underwear. Bright red *Calvin Klein* briefs.

I couldn't help but stare at his body. Jason was in very good shape, with slightly more body hair than I. His pecs were covered with a dusting of red hair, extending down to his navel. His tan was apparently complete as well—no *farmer's tan* for him, despite how often he was working outside in his tee-shirt. *Did he ditch the shirt when I wasn't around?* If he was, then the local housewives certainly weren't complaining. The battery-operated lantern gave off just enough light for me to see the outline of his cock and balls through the cotton. I quickly looked away when Jason glanced at me, hoping he wouldn't notice my staring.

I was glad that I was wearing boxers for sleeping. Right now, though, I was giving serious thought about keeping my shorts and tee-shirt on. My dick was half-erect and getting harder.

Jason didn't seem to notice it though. He climbed into his sleeping bag and laid his head on the pillow. "You sleeping like that?" he asked.

"Course not." I quickly stripped off my own clothes, trying to keep my back to him so that he wouldn't notice the bulge in the front of my boxers.

It was a fairly hot summer evening—between the temperature and the sight of my hunky neighbor, I was feeling way too hot to want to be covered up—so I lay on top of the sleeping bag. I certainly wasn't ashamed of my body as I had a good build and kept myself in shape. I just wanted to hide my erection.

I turned the light off and tried to fall asleep. It wasn't going to be easy. Not with him laying so close to me. Within arm's reach. I could hear him breathing.

"Crap." From the sounds, Jason was trying to crawl out of his sleeping bag.

"What?" I asked as I clicked the lantern back on.

"Call of nature."

"Oh." I was staring at his ass as he climbed to his feet. It was definitely his best feature, strong and round, filling out his underwear. I also got a quick glance of the front of his well-packed briefs as he made his way out of the tent. *Don't you want shorts or something?* I thought about asking.

"I'll be right back."

"Okay." I was hard again. *Yep, he's certainly not shy.* I rolled over onto my stomach. *Don't want to see me all worked up over him. Just freak him out.* I shifted positions, trying to get a bit more comfortable—no easy feat given how hard my cock currently was. *Do I have time to jerk-off?*

Jason popped back through the tent flap, stumbling slightly as he turned to refasten the zip. He ended up losing his balance and landing partially on top of me.

"Geez...I'm sorry," he apologized.

"It's all right." The feel of his almost-naked body was electric, and my own body responded with a full fledged erection—so much for getting soft. I fumbled for the lantern as he climbed off of me; I wanted the light out to avoid detection.

"Sorry about landing on you like that. I lost my balance."

"It's okay," I repeated.

"It's so dark out there...coming back into the light kind of blinded me."

"Oh...from your entrance, I thought maybe someone had seen you streaking through the woods."

"Not a chance." He laughed softly. "Anyway, these are respectable enough. No worse than a *Speedo*."

I couldn't argue with that.

"This whole trip is great! I love camping."

"Didn't you get your fill of that while on tour?"

"It's not the same." There was a pause. "No one around here is shooting at you," he added after a long pause.

"I hadn't thought of that." I kept my voice low. *Open mouth, insert foot.* "I love the outdoors," I said, trying to change the subject. "I can feel the fresh air in my lungs and the blood pumping through my veins."

"Yeah, I noticed!"

I heard the amusement in his voice and felt my face get hot.

"Sorry. I didn't mean to embarrass you, Scott. It just happens to all of us. I mean, you should've seen the number of guys who popped wood in the barracks. Or in the showers. You just get used to seeing them...you ignore them after a while."

Tell me more! I thought.

Sadly, Jason didn't say anything else.

The silence dragged out, until he began to snore. Listening to the sound, I finally fell asleep.

Chapter Eleven

The following morning dawn bright and surprisingly cool.

It was a real scramble to get dressed while desperately needing to find a bathroom. My usual morning hard-on certainly didn't help—and I couldn't very well jerk-off with Jason laying there next to me. I certainly thought about it though. Finally, I rolled out of the sleeping bag, then quickly yanked my jeans on. I pulled a tee-shirt over my head. As I slipped my feet into sandals and scrambled through the tent flap, I noticed that Jason was doing the same—and was apparently having some difficulty working his zipper over his own morning hard-on.

Happens to all of us, right?

We walked together through the forest towards the closest outhouse.

"You didn't walk all this way last night," I said. "You weren't gone long enough."

"No, last night I just wandered a few meters into the forest and found a tree." He had a big grin on his face. "It's good to be a guy."

I shook my head.

From past visits, I knew that the outhouse facilities were located conveniently through the area, though far enough from the campsites to avoid unpleasant smells. This particular building was large enough to offer two urinals and a stall on the guys' side.

As we stood side by side at the urinals, I tried to look only at the wall, but I'm certainly not made of stone. Of course I couldn't help but sneak a quick peek in his direction. My jaw dropped when I saw him holding a good six inches of spongy manhood.

Holy shit! He really was packing those briefs!

Our business done, we walked back to the campsite.

"You know what?"

"What?" I asked. I was wishing I'd thought to grab my hat and sunglasses. The morning sun was very bright.

"We should have brought a bucket with us."

I looked at Jason in confusion for a minute, but then it dawned on me what he meant. "Oh yeah, we're the water boys."

"Yep." He nodded his head. "Now we have to walk back this way.

The others were apparently still asleep when we returned to our campsite.

Jason snatched up four empty water jugs from beside the car. Each one had a handle. "Should be easier to carry these than a bucket," he said.

"Yeah, good thinking."

"Mom's idea. She bought them to make wine—faster than filtering water through the *Brita*. She saved them for when we go camping. Lids and everything so the water won't get bugs in it."

"She thinks of everything, doesn't she?"

We walked through the dirt road. There were a few other tents set up, but none of them were close by us.

Lots of privacy, I noted. That was a good thing...I hated camping when you had other people crowded close by. Part of the thrill being in the woods was getting away from other people.

* * *

Jessica was up and waiting for us when we got back. "Good, you remembered the water." She smiled. "Now I can start breakfast."

"I'd forgotten just how loud that pump was," I said. "We pumped for ages before anything came up."

Jessica laughed. "It's old," she said. "That pump was there when I was a kid and fetching water for my parents. With an old pail, I might add. Not a jug." Still grumbling about the *good old days,* she cooked a nice breakfast for us. Hot coffee first, then she used a cast iron frying pan to fry bacon and eggs over the fire. We even had toast—by holding our bread on sticks in front of the flames.

"Primitive, but still good," Mike commented as he refilled his coffee mug. He drank it black.

"The roar of the raging fire is the perfect spice."

"What are your plans?" Jessica asked. She had just returned the cream to the ice-filled cooler. "I'm going down to the beach to sunbathe for the day. I want to work on my tan. I told the girls at work I was going to come back looking like I'd been to Jamaica."

Mike was nodding his head.

I wasn't surprised. Whenever she went sunbathing in her skimpy bikini, he wouldn't leave her side for fear of some guy hitting on her. He had a bit of a jealous streak—I was certainly no threat to him or her.

"I'm going swimming," Sarah informed us.

"Are you two going fishing?" Mike asked his son.

"I was thinking about going for a hike," Jason said. "A little cross-country walk would be fun. Maybe do some bird watching." He glanced at me.

I frowned. *Why is he looking at me like that?*

"Well, don't get lost," Jessica said.

"Mom!"

"You heard me. This might be a campground, but it's still forest. Anything could be out there. Wolves. Bears."

I've encountered a few bears in my time, I thought. *But there won't be any of* them *around here.*

"I survived my tour overseas," Jason was complaining loudly. "I came home in one piece!"

"And I don't want to see you get mauled now!"

He rolled his eyes.

"If you don't mind the company, I'd like to go with you."

Jason turned towards me with a big smile on his face. "Yeah, I'd like that."

Mike frowned. "I thought you'd want to be at the beach."

"There's plenty of time for that later."

Jessica nodded. "It would be safer with two of you. I can trust Scott to look after you."

"Mom!"

Mike laughed.

"Dad!"

"Hey, while she's bugging you, she's leaving me alone. Right, Scott?"

"Right." I had to laugh as well.

Jason snorted.

We finished our breakfast and then prepared for the planned hike. We packed a backpack with a lunch and some small water bottles.

We also changed—separately this time—into loose tee-shirts and shorts. I was a bit disappointed when Jason didn't immediately follow me back into the tent to change. *I guess I can't have everything*, I thought.

"Have fun!" Mike called out. He was wearing swim trunks and a loose tee-shirt.

Jessica was wearing her infamous red and green bikini, with a towel wrapped sarong-style around her waist.

Even I had to stare.

She gave me a grin. "I must be doing something right if I got *your* attention."

Mike rolled his eyes.

Jason grabbed my hand. "Come on."

Jason and I didn't plan to hike too far away, but we were both ready to wander a bit...and the extra supplies were just a precaution.

"We can't get too lost," Jason pointed out as we made our way down one of the trails. "We go south and hit the lake. We go north to hit the highway. East or west will eventually hit fence line or something. The campsite isn't *that* isolated. Not like we're out in the middle of a desert or something."

"True," I agreed.

The day was getting quite hot. I was glad that I had changed from my jeans to shorts.

I was glad that Jason had changed out of his jeans as well—he had really nice legs and I enjoyed looking at them.

Jason was as excited as a schoolboy by our hike. He kept pointing out various birds in the trees. "Look, a cardinal. Look, a blue jay!"

I was really hoping he did notice how much I was staring at him. I don't think he did, though.

We stopped by one of the countless streams which flowed through the forest down to the lake.

"How about lunch?" Jason asked.

"Sounds like a plan."

We were stopped by a fairly large pool of water. I took off my sneakers, enjoying the feeling of the thick grass and moss on the bottoms of my feet.

I opened one of our water bottles and took a long drink. It was lukewarm, but still refreshing.

"We've got some sandwiches and some trail mix," Jason announced as he dug through the pack.

"Good enough," I told him.

After we ate, I waded into the water to cool off my feet.

Jason soon joined me. The rocky bottom made for nice and clear water, and I was soon contemplating a quick dip to cool off. "Hey Jason, I'm thinking about taking a quick swim. Want to join me?"

"Sure, that sounds great." He paused, with that grin on his face again. "I wish I'd thought to bring my trunks, but it seems pretty secluded." He waded back towards the bank and began to undress.

This is going to be great! I followed him back to shore, lifting off my tee-shirt. I fully expected him to stop stripping at his underwear and just go swimming in his bright red *Calvin Klein* briefs. *No worse than a Speedo, he'd said.* I was looking forward to seeing how the wet cotton would cling to his dick.

Jason surprised me when he peeled off his *Calvins* and turned to enter the water. I saw that his tan lines did follow his underwear. He didn't try to cover his dick either. It swung from side-to-side as he walked towards the water.

Holy shit! I could feel my pulse quickening and my heart rate speed up as I followed his example. My own dick twitched inside my shorts.

He dove into the water and resurfaced. "It does feel great!" he called back to me. "You coming in, or you just gonna stand there and watch?"

"I'm coming." I already had my tee-shirt off and I was undoing my shorts. I let them drop onto the ground, along with my boxers. I strolled towards the water's edge, trying to look and act as unconcerned about my nudity as Jason had done.

And trying not to draw any attention to my semi-hard dick.

If Jason noticed it, he didn't comment.

It was very invigorating to be skinny-dipping. I felt alive. The combination of the cool water, the warm summer sun, and just the overall freedom of being naked.

The water in the pool was just deep enough for some underwater swimming, though not deep enough to provide cover should anyone discover us. Not that either of us cared about passersby. It was a semi-private campground after all, not a public park.

We were far too concerned with splashing each other in our new found boyhood. The splashing grew into dunking, and we were soon wrestling with each other.

I felt Jason swim between my legs and attempt to catch me off guard and dunk me. I felt his hair, and then his back touch my balls, and I shivered with excitement, lost my balance and went under. I came up spitting water, and quickly hurried after him to get him back.

I tried a frontal approach, but was unable to lift him. I dove back underwater and Jason caught me between his legs before I could swim through. I couldn't help but notice the hard-on he had grown.

Of course, by this point in the game, I had an impressive one of my own bouncing off my thighs.

Our little match had become decidedly more sexual as we grappled with one another, trying to manage a dunk.

Finally having had enough, I evaded his grasp and hurried back to the shore. Our horseplay had moved us downstream from our picnic area. This patch of shoreline was quite muddy. I scooped up a handful and threw it, hitting Jason square in the chest.

He looked surprised by that, but he recovered quickly and gave me a grin before trying to tackle me.

I kept my balance that time.

The mud was really gooey and slimy. It was impossible to keep our footing and we were quickly covered in mud from head to foot. Both of us were still rock-hard as well as we kneeled in the mud.

I scooped up another handful of mud and splattered it against Jason's cock.

He didn't try to stop me either. He just grunted and his eyes rolled back.

Now it was my turn to be surprised. His cock was warm to my touch, and the shaft was smooth, the head nicely shaped. I squished the brown mud into his balls and coated the shaft.

"Mmph." Jason spread his legs and I rammed mud everywhere, even teasing his asshole.

He returned the favor, coating my dick and balls with mud. His hands felt so wonderful as he fondled me.

The sexual energy between us was intense.

And he was my employee, I thought. *My neighbor's son.* "We should stop," I said, trying to pull away from him.

He stared at me with those beautiful brown eyes. "It's too late now." He continued coating my dick with mud, stroking me.

"No, fuck!" I cried out as I lost control of myself. The mud acted as a lubricant and Jason stroked me to a climax before I even realized how close I was. "Fuck!" I grunted again as I shot my load.

Jason was grinning.

Gasping for breath, I looked down at myself. Ropes of white cum coated my dick, stomach, and chest. It contrasted sharply with the brown mud. "Shit." I looked at Jason, thoroughly embarrassed by this.

Jason was still kneeling beside me. His own erection was standing out, bobbing as he shifted positions. "Nice one, Scott."

I closed my eyes for a moment. *Maybe this was all some dream!* "I'm sorry, Jason. I never planned to—"

"Who gives a fuck?" he countered. "Don't worry, that mud fight was pretty wild. There's only one problem now..."

I followed his gaze down to his own erection. I felt my face redden even more. I quickly cleared my throat. "I'll go and get cleaned up while you finish."

"What's your rush?" He scooped some of the muddy cum from my stomach and smeared it onto his own dick. He didn't say another word, but laid down in the mud and openly stroked himself.

I stared, unable to look away. I knew I should, but seeing him naked and wet had been the fulfillment of so many fantasies. Now he was jerking off right beside me. Part of me wanted to reach over and help him.

Jason was grunting softly as he played with himself. His eyes were half-closed, his mouth half-open, his breath coming in quick pants. "Ugh!" He didn't shoot very far, but the cum which pooled on lower stomach came in a surprisingly big amount.

Without a word, I hurried back into the water to clean myself off.

He followed me.

Still silent, we got dressed in our shorts and tee-shirts and resumed the hike.

Walking through the woods, I found it very hard to look Jason in the eye. *How did I let things go that far? What would Mike say?* Not that I expected Jason to mention the afternoon's horseplay to his folks.

We returned to the campsite.

Jessica and Mike were inside their tent. It was zipped up. There was no sign of Sarah.

Jason was refilling his water bottle from one of the jugs. "You want some?" he asked.

"Sure." I felt awkward.

Mike came out of the tent. He was wearing his nylon swim trunks and nothing else. He had a nice hairy chest, though it showed more gray than his hair. I thought I could see his dick, outlined against the material as he walked towards us.

"How was your hike?" he asked.

"Good," Jason replied. "Tiring, but fun."

"See any bears?"

"Nope."

Mike looked at me. "Did he wear you out?" he asked.

"What? No, not at all." I heard the panic in my voice, though Mike didn't seem to notice. "It was a fun. We hiked. We went for a swim in one of the streams."

Mike gave me a wink. "Took the boy skinny-dipping, did you?" His chuckle was loud. "Don't worry, I won't tell your mother."

Jason rolled his eyes.

I hastily took another drink of water and wished that it had something strong and alcoholic mixed into it.

Chapter Twelve

Nightfall saw us back around the campfire. Sarah had caught some small trout in the lake and we were enjoying them.

Jason had changed from his shorts into fleece sweatpants now that the sun was going down. Even though it was now July, it was still cool.

I had put some nylon track pants on as well.

We talked for hours. Mike asked how well Jason was doing as my main worker. I answered truthfully—Jason was a hard worker and quick to learn.

Jessica laughed at that. "He never liked cutting our lawn," she announced. "We always had to bribe him."

"That's because it was *our* lawn," he told her. "When it's someone else's that makes all the difference."

"Oh."

All too soon it had grown late and it was time to turn in. The fire had gone out, and Mike drowned the ashes with the last of our water. "You two can go and pump some more tomorrow morning." He headed into his tent.

Jason and I sat quietly on the ground. I didn't want to be the first to move. *This isn't going to go well,* I thought.

Jason was staring towards the lake. We could just see it from our campsite, the dark water glistening in spots as the waves caught moonlight.

Finally I stood up, stretching to relieve some of the stiffness I felt. I wandered a short distance away from camp, stepping behind a nearby tree to empty my bladder. The bathrooms were too far away to bother with.

I had the front of my pants pulled down and my dick hanging out, but before I could begin, I heard a branch snap.

I twisted my head around.

Jason stepped around the tree. "There you are." He stopped beside me. "I figured this was what you were doing." He lowered his own sweatpants and pulled out his cock to pee.

Hearing his stream hit the ground was enough to trigger my own.

We finished at the same time and he put himself away.

I was trying not to look. I put myself back into my boxers and pulled my pants up. *This afternoon was a mistake. No we have to live with it.*

Jason headed for our tent.

I followed, slowly. "I'll just grab my sleeping bag and go crash under a bush."

He paused at the flap and looked back at me. "What are you talking about?"

"I didn't think you wanted me sleeping in there."

"Of course I want you to sleep with me." He was smiling, his teeth bright in the moonlight.

I stared at him.

He vanished into the tent. After a moment, I heard his voice again. "You coming in or what?"

I pushed through the flap and into the lantern-lit tent. It was going to be another fun night of changing our clothes in the confined space. Bumping our bodies together.

I've already seen him naked, I thought. *I've seen him shoot his load...why should simply being alone with him to strip down for bed be so nerve wracking?*

Jason already had his tee-shirt pulled off. He gave me a grin, then slid his track pants down. He was wearing black *Calvin Klein* briefs this time.

Suppressing a sigh, I stripped off my own tee-shirt and dropped my pants. Once again, my dick was half-erect and getting harder.

Jason was laying on top of his sleeping bag. He was watching me get undressed.

That made my dick twitch inside my purple *Hanes* boxer briefs.

I thought about diving into my sleeping bag and hiding in it. I knew that I was showing a bulge.

Jason was still smiling. "I wanted to talk to you, Scott."

"I'm sorry about the mud wrestling thing." I kept my voice as low as his was—I was pretty sure that neither of us wanted his parents to overhear.

"Don't be sorry. That was incredible."

"It was?"

"Hell yeah. I've been skinny-dipping before, and I was in the army so being naked around other guys isn't anything new to me. But that mud fight was something else. You pushed me into overdrive."

"Uh...."

"It was awesome."

I rolled onto my stomach, to try and hide my all-too-obvious hard-on.

"I know you're gay, Scott."

My breath caught in my throat.

"We all know it. You've never really tried to hide it from us."

"It just never comes up in conversations." That was the honest truth.

"Mom thinks you're hot."

"God."

"I heard her talking to some of her friends one time. It was a girls night or something—Dad had already left and I was waiting for my buddies to come and pick me up. They were in the living room talking. They'd already had a few drinks, and one of the ladies saw you through the window. You were getting out of your truck, I think. She commented on how what a cutie you were.

"Mom said it was a waste, cause you played for the other team. They all laughed and a few asked for your number. They wanted to try and convert you."

I shook my head. "So that's where all those calls came from." I remembered those women. Half a dozen of them hiring me to look after their yards...and trying to seduce me.

"I agreed with her. You are a *cutie*...and it's not a waste."

I froze, unable to breath.

"I know about Uncle Alec. I know he's gay. The whole family knows that." Jason had left his sleeping bag and now he sat down next to me. "You two went to college together."

"That was ten years ago."

"So did you and he ever...." His voice trailed off into an uncomfortable silence.

Finally, I lifted my head looked at him. "Is that really any of your business?"

"Did you and my uncle have sex?"

"Does it matter?"

"Do you think I'm hot?"

"What?"

"Am I as hot as Uncle Alec?" Jason prompted. "I mean, he looks good. I know I shouldn't think that way, but *he* is a wet-dream."

I was shocked hearing this.

"If he wasn't my uncle, I'd jump him in an instant." Jason lowered his voice even more. "I like older guys. It's my weakness."

I twisted my head to look at him. I was staring right into Jason's crotch. His briefs were tenting outwards.

Jason was looking right at me. "So, do you think I'm hot?"

"Yes," I replied honestly. I shifted positions on the sleeping bag, trying to get a bit more comfortable. With him right there, it wasn't easy.

Jason reached out and rolled me over. "Ah-ha!"

My own arousal was pretty obvious.

"I've watched you when we're working," Jason continued softly. "I've seen you looking at me."

"I—"

"I've enjoyed it. Scott, asked to work for you because I knew you would enjoy watching me. And because I knew I'd enjoy watching you. Fuck, you're a hunk and I've wanted to have you for months. Years."

"Years?"

"I knew I was gay before I enlisted. Shit, I used to lay in bed and jerk-off at night thinking about you. You have no idea how many tissues I'd go through in a week. You'd come over for dinner or we'd go to your place and that night I would shoot three or four times."

I shook my head.

"I was the one who suggested to Mom and Dad about inviting you along camping. I was thrilled when you agreed. I was hoping for something like the pond. To get you skinny-dipping at least. So I could see your entire body."

"I trust it didn't disappoint."

"It was more than I imagined." He ran his fingers down the front of his briefs. "I couldn't resist jerking-off back there." Now he reached for the front of my boxer briefs and stroked my obvious shaft.

My entire body shivered. "Jason, I'm not sure about this."

"What? I'm twenty-one. I'm an adult. I'm not a virgin either...I've had multiple guys."

What an odd thing to boast about. "What about your parents?"

"They know I'm gay. I told them before I went to boot camp."

"They *know*?" But did they have any idea that their son and their neighbor were having an affair? *A real family affair*, I thought, thinking about my occasional sexual romps with Alec.

Jason was still stroking me.

"We should stop."

"Why?"

"Because...fuck. I'm your employer. I'm older than you."

"Ten years. Big deal."

"I'm your—" I couldn't finish my sentence because Jason leaned down and kissed me.

"I want you, Scott." He kissed me again. "I want you so badly." His briefs had a glistening patch on them, where he was leaking pre-cum. "Right here, right now."

"I...I...shit." I nodded, unable to muster any other arguments or willingness to play any more games. "I want to fuck your tight ass so badly!"

A big grin split Jason's face. "Good." We kissed again. His hands slid down to my waist. "Let's get rid of these." He pulled my boxer briefs down, the front briefly snagging on my erection. His hand lingered momentarily on my hardness, then continued to slide my underwear further down my legs.

Jason pulled off his own briefs, letting his hard-on spring out.

"Damn, that's a nice sight."

He lay down on his sleeping bag and I straddled him, my ass rubbing into the cleft of his ass-cheeks.

I rubbed my hands along his back, feeling his muscles under my fingers, feeling my hard cock slide between our bodies. I moved lower to massage his calves, returning

upwards to his thigh. I desperately wanted to explore his ass.

As if he could read my mind, he spread his legs.

I licked my index finger and moved it along the crack to his hole.

I knew Jason was enjoying this by both his soft moaning and by the way he pushed against my finger. I wanted to be gentle, but part of me was still caught up in the frenzy of the moment.

Jason had raised himself to his knees, and his balls were dangling freely. My finger was still probing into him. I shifted positions, rubbing my dick up and down along his ass.

"Fuck me," Jason prompted.

"I don't have any lube," I replied. "I didn't pack anything like that."

"Right front pocket." Jason was reaching for his discarded shorts. The same ones he'd worn hiking earlier that day. "Front pocket."

I reached for them. My dick rubbed against his ass, teasing the hole and almost popping in. I pulled the shorts to me. Lube and two condoms.

"I was military," he told me. "I'm prepared for anything."

"Good to know."

I tore open the condom and put it on. Then I squeezed lube onto my dick. "Brace yourself." I pressed my dick against his ass, feeling the resistance from his hole.

Jason pushed back against me, and the head of my dick popped inside. He gasped once.

I remained still. He'd claimed to have multiple guys, but how many had he really had sex with? How many had topped him?

A few seconds passed before Jason pushed again. I suddenly felt the warmth and silkiness of being inside him. It was stimulating and arousing and every bit as enjoyable as fucking his uncle. I began with slow, easy strokes.

When I felt him relax, I began to fuck him in earnest. My balls were slapping against his ass. I held his hips in my hands as I began to feel that familiar response inside me. I tried to be quiet, but made a deep groan as I shot my load.

Panting, I slowly pulled myself back out.

Jason rolled over so I could see his face. There were tears on his cheeks.

"Shit! Did I hurt you?"

"No, it was great." He leaned forward and kissed me. "It was even better than I dreamed it would be."

I blinked.

"Way better than five years of bed-time fantasies." He kissed me again.

I could feel his own hard-on rubbing against my stomach now. "That's right, you haven't cum yet." I lowered my head, first sucking his nipples, then moving further down to his cock. His pre-cum was slick on my tongue, and I worked my way around his head, stopping to probe his slit.

Jason responded by laying back down and moaning softly. I sucked on his balls, taking them into my mouth. I moved to his dick, my free hands moving upwards to play with his nipples, and I kept sucking him.

"I'm gonna cum!" he grunted. "Fuck!"

The first gush of cum was overwhelming and it flooded my mouth. The second almost made me choke and I pulled back just in time for the third to splash down my chin. I'd forgotten just how much he shot!

I blinked at him as he lay there.

He opened his beautiful eyes and looked at me. Then he started to laugh. "You look like you slopped a milkshake on your face."

"Thanks." I scooped my tee-shirt from the floor of the tent and used it to wipe off my face. I also pulled the condom off my still semi-hard dick and wiped it clean. The tee-shirt would be fine after washing...if not, it was one of my good ones.

Jason kissed me again. There was no wild passion in this one, but it was a deep and meaningful one.

Chapter Thirteen

We fell asleep like that, cuddled in each other's arms. When I awoke, the sun was

already warming the tent. I almost didn't remember where I was.

Then it all came flooding back to me.

It was the morning after I'd had sex with my neighbor's son.

His adult and fully grown-up son, I had to admit. I could feel *his* hard-on pressing into my stomach. Morning wood...nothing quite like it. I had one of my own pressing against his thigh.

I was in the crook of Jason's arms, wrapped in a sleeping bag.

Jason mumbled something.

I stared at him. *What will his parents say?* What if Mike or Jessica stuck their heads into our tent? Jason and I were naked, sharing one sleeping bag. I tried to think of some rational and believable reason for this situation. *I've got nothing.*

"Good morning."

I looked at the man in my arms.

Jason's eyes were half-open. "I had the greatest dream last night," he announced in a sleepy voice.

"Really?"

"You were amazing last night." He pressed his body against me, making sure I could feel his hardness. "You gonna let this go to waste?" He had taken a firm grip on my dick with his hand.

"It'll go limp soon enough," I told him.

"It's more fun to use it." He threw the sleeping bag away from us, exposing our flesh to the cool morning air. He reached for the discarded bottle of lube from last night. He squeezed some into his hand and began to stroke me.

I tried to protest, tried to mention that his folks were probably up by now, but I gave up. It was more important for me to keep my lips tightly shut and prevent myself from crying out as I approached orgasm.

Jason had learned how to stroke cock with the best and I groaned in pleasure.

All too quickly, it was over—my cum was splattered on my stomach and I was slumped on my back.

Jason grinned. "You seemed to enjoy that."

"I did." I reached over and let my hand brush across his chest. His nipples responded to my touch, growing hard. There was still flakes of dried cum in his chest hair. My hand moved down his torso. Jason's dick was rock-hard as I gripped it in my hand and stroked it gently.

He spread his legs, and rolled his head back, closing his eyes.

I reached for the lube and squirted some onto my hand. I went back to stroking his shaft, while I used my free hand to play with his balls.

It took only a few minutes before he groaned and shot a load of cum over my hand. God, did he always shot gallons?

"What are you doing to me?" he asked. "Wasn't last night enough?"

"No, I guess not." I gave him a grin. "You wanted this to happen...don't complain when your wishes come true."

"I see that you're up as well." He reached down and gave my dick a squeeze. "You want to try round two?"

"No. We need to get up before you folks walk in on us." I used my already cum-stained tee-shirt to clean us both off.

"I need to take a leak," Jason announced.

"Yeah, me too."

We rolled over, in opposite directions, and both of us reached for some fresh clothes.

* * *

Jason was looking rugged now. He hadn't shaved in three days and the stubble on his face gave him a scruffy and sexy look.

Of course, that look was shared by Mike and myself. Mike made scruffy look as good as his son.

Jason told me I looked sexy with the stubble.

Jessica just rolled her eyes and made comments about living with unwashed barbarians.

It's not that we weren't clean per se. We all had been swimming in the lake, with biodegradable soap, but it wasn't the same as taking a hot shower.

Mike just found it amusing. "We came to get away from civilization," he commented. "Now you bitch that you'd don't have your creature comforts."

"It wasn't me who spent an hour last night moaning about how good a *Timmie's* coffee would taste."

Mike's jaw dropped.

"Score one for mom," Sarah giggled.

Jessica had a big grin on her face.

"I have no idea what you are talking about," Mike announced. He turned to the supplies and began rummaging through the cans. "Where is that instant coffee?"

I was pretty sure they had no idea that their son and I were having sex in the tent every night.

Every *night?* Hell, we kept sneaking off during the day to fool around. I don't know how many blow jobs we gave each other, hiding in the bushes away from the campsite, or else stopping on our daily afternoon hikes. We returned to our private picnic spot three times to skinny-dip. And we had sex there every single time.

I was impressed by how many condoms Jason had brought along with him. I was equally impressed by how much stamina he possessed. I had never met anyone who was as constantly horny as me...but I was now thinking that he was going to wear me out.

* * *

"That was fun." I lifted my duffle bag out of the back of Mike's station wagon. "I really enjoyed the weekend."

Mike gave me a pleased smile—he had the same smile as Jason. "You want to come over for a barbeque tonight?"

"Actually, I think I'm gonna order a pizza."

"A *pizza*?"

"Yeah, I've had my fill of fire-cooking for now."

He laughed. "Suit yourself."

"Right now, I really need a nice hot shower."

"Yeah, that is one thing I do miss." Mike nodded his head. "If you change your mind, feel free to pop over."

"I'll think about it."

There was no sign of Jason. He'd grabbed his stuff and vanished into the house. I wondered if the ride home had been too *stimulating* for him. Body contact had been unavoidable in the back seat.

How is this going to affect our relationship? I knew that it would change things. Sex always did. *What happened on vacation was simply what happened on vacation. We're home now and back to our real lives.* That made sense.

I unlocked the door and went inside my house.

I dropped my duffle onto the kitchen table. The phone was flashing so I hit the answering machine *play* button. Wrong number, job inquiry which I noted the number down to call back later, telemarketer, some friends looking to meet for a movie on Friday. I was never more popular than when I wasn't at home.

I carried the duffle downstairs to the laundry room. I opened it and started filling the washer. I shook my cum-stained tee-shirt out, smiled, and tossed it into the sudsy water. I stripped off the clothes I was wearing to add to the load, then headed upstairs with my mostly empty duffle.

Someone knocked at the side door.

Talk about timing. I shook my head and looked around. "Hang on!" I called. I ducked into the bedroom and grabbed my bathrobe off its hook on the door. I hurried back across the house as whomever was out there knocked a second time. I was just tying the sash when I reached the door.

I turned the knob and opened it.

Jason was standing outside. His eyes lit up as he took in the sight of me wearing only a loose terrycloth robe. "Can I come in?" he asked. He had found time to clean up—he was dressed in the ratty dark green tee-shirt and cut-off denim shorts he'd worn when we painted the living room—and shave.

"Sure, come on in." I stepped aside, then closed the door. "What's up?"

"I wanted to talk to you…without my parents around to overhear us."

"Okay." I scratched myself. "Can it wait until after I take a shower? I swear I still have mud drying on me inner thighs."

He grinned. "Go ahead."

I rolled my eyes and headed upstairs to my bathroom. I could hear him following me. "What did you want to talk about?"

"Us."

"Oh." I paused before untying my robe. Jason had followed me to the bathroom, standing in the doorway, and watching. He had an almost challenging expression on his face.

Muttering '*ah fuck it*', I let the bathrobe fall open and I shrugged out of it. *Not like he hasn't seen all this before,* I thought to myself.

Jason certainly acted like he hadn't seen it before. His eyes roamed up and down my body.

I actually felt dirty. "You're acting like you're undressing me with your eyes."

"You're not wearing clothes," he countered.

I started the shower.

Jason was still watching.

I stepped into the tub and closed the glass door. I sighed as the hot water flooded across my body. It felt *so* damned good. I reached for the shampoo and lathered up my hair. I squeezed some body wash gel onto a facecloth and began to soap up my chest.

I thought I heard Jason moan, but I had soap in my eyes and kept them squeezed shut.

While soaping my balls and ass, I began to feel myself growing aroused. I knew Jason was watching me, but I didn't care. I was horny and I wanted to release the tension. I ran the soapy cloth across my groin again, working up a lather while stroking myself into a semi-hard state.

"You have mud on your back."

I jumped as I felt hands brush against me.

My eyes snapped open.

Jason had stripped off his clothes and joined me in the shower. "Let me get it for it," he said as he took the face cloth out of my hand.

His gentle touch felt so nice against my skin, my body responded by stiffening to full attention.

Jason chuckled. "I thought we took care of this earlier?" He gave my hard dick a squeeze.

"That was hours ago," I replied.

"I guess we should make sure it's good and clean then."

I felt his hands go lower on my back, and suddenly he was caressing my ass. I spread my legs in an automatic response. I could feel Jason's hands slide lower and lower. My dick was rock-hard now, and I could feel Jason's own hard-on brushing against me.

He was very thorough, working that soapy cloth all over my body.

"You look clean now."

I turned towards him. Our hard cocks touched.

He was smiling.

"And are you clean?" I asked him.

"Want to examine me?" Jason turned and spread his legs while holding his hands against the wall.

He was definitely being provocative and I wanted him. My dick was sore and aching—I was that hard.

I soaped up my hands and moved closer to him. I ran my fingers along his back, like I had done in the tent that second night, working my way lower down. I lathered up with more soap and began to massage his ass cheeks. I could see his balls, and I reached down to stroke them.

He wiggled his butt at me.

I brushed a single finger down his crack, to his hole, and Jason tensed.

The spray from the shower was rinsing the soap off of us both.

Jason turned around, his erection bouncing.

We were both hard and aroused.

Using the soap as an excuse, I lathered up his chest and stomach. The light dusting of reddish hair was silky beneath my hands.

Jason closed his eyes and tilted his head back. As I made contact with his pubes, the veins in his cock throbbed. I soaped up his balls, making it a slow and sensual wash instead of utilitarian. My own inhibitions were no longer a factor...we were both consenting adults in a private home.

I finally took a soapy grip on his dick—Jason groaned at that—beginning a slow but steady pumping action with my fist. I increased speed, his groans almost drowned out by the shower. His knees buckled as he shot his load.

The cum splashed my leg and was immediately washed away by the warm water.

"You...against the wall," he gasped. He pushed me against the wall, soaping up my own groin and fondling my dick and balls.

I closed my eyes in pleasure, enjoying the feel of his hand on my dick. Then his hand was removed and water splashed across my private parts. I waited with my eyes closed him to resume his hand-job.

A warm and moist touch made me open my eyes and look down.

Jason was on his knees, my cock in his mouth.

"Oh, fuck," I said. He was really skilled at what he was doing. I relied on the wall of the tub for support. The blow-job was that intense and pleasurable. I felt that familiar tenseness in my balls. "I'm gonna—" I began, but my warning came too late.

Jason gagged as the first volley of cum filled his mouth, but he didn't move away until I was done shooting.

With towels wrapped around our waists, we stumbled into my bedroom.

Jason looked around, seeing it for the first time. One wall was covered with pictures printed off the net of various guys I considered hot, in various provocative poses and states of undress.

I collapsed onto my bed with a loud groan. "I could sleep for a week." The pillows felt so soft and the mattress was so welcoming. *Am I getting too old for camping?*

Jason glanced at me. "You just had a vacation."

"And tomorrow it's back to work." I gave him a weak smile. "For us both, buddy, in case you forgot." I half expected him to announce that he was going to quit.

He moved to sit on the edge of the bed. His towel slipped, but he didn't bother to adjust it. "Are we working together on each job, or are we splitting up to do two at once?"

"Uh...I forget what I have planned." I really wasn't sure. "Should be mostly lawn cutting and shrub pruning. We both work at each job and it'll be done in no time."

He nodded.

I closed my eyes.

I felt the bed shake and I opened my eyes.

Jason was moving. He had dropped his towel onto the floor and was now crawling up next to me.

"What are you—"

"Just getting comfortable." He was untying my towel and tugging at it.

With a sigh, I lifted my ass up so he could finish pulling the towel free. Then he snuggled up next to me. *Not again,* I thought.

But he didn't seem interested in another round of sex...he just wanted to snuggle.

I had to admit, I did enjoy having his naked body pressed against mine.

Chapter Fourteen

I opened my eyes.

It was dark

"Jason?"

He blinked his eyes and sat up. "What?"

"It's dark." I looked for my watch. "What time is it?"

"Can't be that late." Jason rolled out of bed and walked towards the window. "I mean, it's July."

My watch said four thirty-seven. My eyes said it had to be after eight.

"It's cloudy." Jason pushed the window open. "Really cloudy."

I got out of bed and walked to the window. "Wow." The sky was indeed overcast. Low-hanging clouds that were blacker than Jason's *Calvin Klein* briefs. "Must be a storm coming in." I could feel the breeze blowing through the now-open window.

"We picked a good day to come home from camping." He chuckled. "We're gonna get a real downpour anytime now."

"Yeah, I think you're right." The trees were blowing back and forth.

The rain was pounding against the glass. One minute it was still and calm, the next the storm had struck with all the fury of a biblical deluge.

Jason shook his head at the sight. "I think I'll stay here for a bit. I'd drown trying to cross the street."

"Do your parents know you're over here?" We were both dressed and sitting down in the living room.

He shook his head. "I told them I was going out for a bit. They probably think I'm out with George and Patrick. Or with Stan...but I don't see him very much now."

A sharp crack of thunder made the house shake.

"Holy shit." Jason looked at me. "I don't like storms."

"No?"

"No." He shook his head. "I used too, when I was kid. Now..." He winced as another crack of thunder boomed. "It's like being overseas."

I nodded my head. "I understand." Like being caught under enemy fire. *Were you in combat?* I'd never heard him mention it. For that matter, I didn't know exactly *what* position he'd had in the army. Basic infantry? Base mechanic?

"I love storms," I told him. "But I can why you don't."

"I like the rain," he said. "I missed that in the desert. It's the thunder I don't like."

Yep, he'd been under enemy fire. "I need a drink. You want something?" I stood up and headed towards the kitchen.

"Yeah...if you don't mind."

"What do you want?"

"What do you have?"

"I'm having a rum-and-Coke. Should still be a few beers in the fridge." I pointed to one of the cupboards. "Help yourself to whatever you want."

He looked inside my erstwhile liquor cabinet. "Rum is good enough."

I poured us two stiff drinks. I made sure they were strong. I suspected he'd need it to get through the storm...and I'd need it to get through our impending conversation. "You hungry? I was thinking about ordering a pizza tonight."

"Pizza is good." He looked out the window as a flash of lightning lit up the street. "But is anyone going to drive in this?"

"Good question." It could wait."

He stuffed his hands into his jeans.

I swear I could see him shivering as the thunder boomed. It made my heart ache.

Jason was staring through the window.

I sighed. *It's going to be a long night.*

We took our drinks back to the living room. I'd decided to order the pizza later in the evening—give the storm time to blow over.

"So...are you seeing anyone?"

I looked at Jason. "Sorry?"

"I should've asked you sooner," he said. "But are you seeing anyone? I mean, after the last few days, I don't think you are. Or you wouldn't have been so quick to jump me in the tent. Or the shower today. But you might be in a long distance—"

"You're rambling."

He closed his mouth.

"I'm not seeing anyone right now," I told him. "No boyfriend. No jealous wife playing the role of my beard and making it look like I'm straight."

Jason laughed, then sipped his drink.

"I'm gay and everyone around knows it. Hell, I think half of my clients know it. Not that it stops the women from staring." I shrugged. "I'm single. Always have been. A few one night stands now and then since college. A few regular fuck-buddies." *Like your uncle,* I thought but I didn't say that out loud. "No one steady."

A fresh peal of thunder boomed.

I paused to take a sip of my drink. "What about you?"

"No one special," Jason said. His drink was half-gone...and I'd been quite generous with the rum. "No boyfriend either. There was this one guy I was stationed with, but that was just overseas action. I haven't played around with Stan since we got back to Canada and mustered out." He shrugged. "He was just a fuck-buddy...it wasn't serious."

"Lonely guys overseas with no easy women?"

"Yeah...for most of them. A lot of playing around in the showers or in the bunks at night. Mostly solo play too—the army had strict rules about sexual contact. Most of us didn't want to take chances while on base. Off-base, on leave...well, that was always a different matter." He took another sip of his drink. "So...where does this leave us?"

"What do you mean?" I asked.

"Is it just sex?"

"Are you asking me to marry you?"

He laughed. "Hardly, Scott," he chuckled. "But I am serious. Was this past week just a vacation fling, or are you and I going to become something more?"

"You mean regular fuck-buddies?"

"I could live with that," he said. "I was hoping to hear that...well, maybe that you wanted to date."

"I'm not sure if we have enough in common to build a relationship," I told him. "I mean, it's got to be based on more than just sex. However amazing the sex has been. We've been eying each other for a while, but lust fades." That was what had happened with his uncle Alec...we were hot for each other in college and then we drifted apart. Now it was just occasional meetings for sex.

"I know."

"We're business partners...can we work together day after day if we're dating? If we have a fight or falling out, that will affect the business."

"I won't let it affect your job, Scott. If we have a falling out, I'll quit. No worries there."

"And think about your parents. Will they be happy if you shack up with me? I enjoy my friendship with them. I don't want to lose it."

"They know that I'm gay," he reminded me. "They know you are too. Anyway, Mom just wants me to be happy."

"And Mike?"

"Dad wants me to happy too. And safe...he gave me that box of condoms I took camping."

I almost choked on my drink. "He *what*?"

"He gave me a box of condoms after I moved back home. He told me he wanted me to be safe. 'You came back alive and unharmed. Why risk catching something now?' I've just been carrying them around ever since."

I shook my head.

More thunder boomed.

"So...how about that pizza?" Jason asked. "I'll buy."

"You're on." I reached for my cell phone. "You got a place you prefer?"

"No, they're all about the same."

"Well I like *Tina's*. It's close by and really good. They always have a great two-for-one deal."

"Sounds good. I like Hawaiian."

"That's good...that's my favourite too."

"That's the best type. Deluxe is nice, but I love pineapple and ham."

* * *

The phone rang.

I picked up my cell phone from the table. "Flat Earth Landscaping," I said into the receiver. "Let us whack your bush into shape." I saved the file I had been working on in case I needed to open a fresh window on my laptop.

"*You sly dog.*"

I frowned. "Alec?"

"*You're fucking my nephew?*"

"How the hell do you know that?" I demanded, too surprised to deny it.

"*He told me.*" Alec was chuckling now. "*He came over last night and asked me flat out if you and I were an item back in college. I told him we were, but it was long ago. He said that was a good thing, cause you were fucking him now.*"

"I feel dirty." I couldn't believe my ears. "I didn't plan on this. I want you to know that. I never planned on seducing your nephew."

"I won't ask if he's any good. I really don't want to know."

"It's none of your business, Alec. Though, I'm not sure if you and I should be seeing each other."

"We shouldn't," he answered bluntly. *"We talked about that the other week. Remember?"*

"I seem to vaguely recall something about that. Before you ripped my suit off, after you ripped my suit off...I do recall talking about our moving on."

"I've got a new guy of my own."

"Oh? Anyone I know?"

"No."

"Is it a *friend*, or something more serious?"

"I don't just have sex with anyone," Alec told me.

"No, you have standards. So, what's his name?"

"Stan Jarvis."

I frowned...I knew that name from somewhere. I concentrated really hard. "The guy renting your basement?"

"Yeah..."

"Wow." I shook my head. "When did all this start?"

"It's been building for a while."

"Do I get the gory details?"

"Nosey, aren't you?"

"Yeah, I am."

"We went to a bar with some buddies of mine. We drank too much. We went home, drank even more, and ended up fucking each other senseless. Cue several weeks of guilt and eventually a reconciliation."

"I know those feelings."

"My nephew has the family stubbornness."

"I've noticed...he takes after you." I paused, holding the phone loosely in my hand. "He also takes after you in the bedroom."

"*I don't need to know that!*"

I laughed.

Alec grunted. "*We should get together and talk.*"

"Dinner?" I asked. "Should I buy a new suit to wear over?"

"*Let's just have pizza or Chinese at your place,*" he said.

There was a knock at my door.

I looked up. I could see Jason waving at me through the window. "I've got company at the door. I'll have to go."

"*All right. Call me with a date and a time.*"

"I'll do that. Maybe you can bring Stan with you. I'll invite Jason and we can all get to know each other."

"*I'll think about it. Bye.*"

"Bye." I clicked the phone off and unlocked the front door.

"Hey there, stud," Jason said leaning over to give me a big kiss.

I returned it with pleasure.

Also by Frank Sol

Novels Of The Sensual City
A Family Affair
Delivering The Goods
Divine Punishment
Good Neighbours
Just Between Friends
Landscaping, Manscaping
Titan's Cradle - A Novel of the Sensual Suns

Novels On The Prairies
Bareback Range
Return To Bareback Range
Fenced In